LUTYENS' MAVERICK

Praise for the Book

'This collection of op-ed essays by Mr Jay Panda puts our professional columnists to shame by comparison. It is astonishing that Mr Panda, a brilliant politician from Odisha, with a national reputation, whom many of us hope and expect to see in high office someday, has found the time to write thoughtful, stylistic and perceptive essays on a vast range of subjects that require our attention. I can only applaud!'

—**Jagdish Bhagwati**
University professor (Economics, Law and
International Affairs), Columbia University

'Jay Panda is an exceptional human being and a gifted parliamentarian. His book has profound insights that can only be acquired through long years of engagement as a grass-roots politician. It is a must-read for anybody who wants to understand the critical intersections of politics and public policy.'

—**Manish Tewari**
Lawyer and national spokesperson, Indian National Congress

'Jay Panda is one of India's thinking politicians. Rather than taking binary positions, he goes into the depth of issues, responds in a thoughtful, nuanced manner and suggests solutions. He has been a staunch supporter of the Aadhaar biometric ID program, while also advocating a strong privacy law.'

—**Nandan Nilekani**
Co-founder, Infosys, and former chairman,
Unique Identification Authority of India (UIDAI)

'Jay Panda is one of those rare politicians who not only speak engagingly and convincingly but also write analytically and fluently. His columns make for compelling reading. I try never to miss them. This book will be very rewarding to read and difficult to put down.'

—**Karan Thapar**
Veteran journalist and commentator

'In his writings, Jay Panda combines the rigour of a researcher with the pragmatism of a practitioner. He writes on the big issues of our times with clarity, and provides a thought-through perspective. He is interested in a wide variety of subjects ranging from traditional wisdom to cutting-edge ideas. Whether you agree or disagree with his conclusions, this book will stimulate your mind.'

—**Haseeb A. Drabu**
Economist and former finance minister, Jammu & Kashmir

LUTYENS' MAVERICK

Ground realities, Hard choices and Tomorrow's India

BAIJAYANT 'JAY' PANDA

RUPA

Published by
Rupa Publications India Pvt. Ltd 2019
7/16, Ansari Road, Daryaganj
New Delhi 110002

Sales Centres:
Allahabad Bengaluru Chennai
Hyderabad Jaipur Kathmandu
Kolkata Mumbai

ISBN: 978-93-5333-343-0

Second impression 2019

10 9 8 7 6 5 4 3 2

The moral right of the author has been asserted.

Printed and bound in India by Gopsons Papers Ltd, Noida

CONTENTS

INTRODUCTION

I have always been an avid reader, thoroughly enjoying Enid Blyton's children's books at age eight and, with equal fascination, having read C. Rajagopalachari's English versions of both the *Mahabharata* and the *Ramayana* by age eleven. This may have had something to do with the legacy of a maternal grandfather who was a professor of history, as well as that of parents, teachers, uncles, aunts, siblings, cousins and friends—many of whom were bibliophiles.

I picked up a sense of curiosity from them. Reading was encouraged in my family, with the exception of mealtimes, but even that restriction was more honoured in the breach. It also helped that I grew up before the age of real television (the single black-and-white government channel did not count) and long before the Internet.

From the racy novels that I read in school along with my friends, my tastes inched up what I considered a ladder of advancement. In college for a technical education, it fell upon me to develop my own tastes, rather than have a large 'required' reading list of the classics. But it somehow always felt incumbent to round off my education with a good dose of voluntary reading material not related to my formal degree.

I developed a taste for non-fiction—history, biographies, science (particularly, with a penchant for evolutionary psychology), economics, social and political commentary, and much more. I also acquired a taste for the kind of professional reportage represented by *The Economist*, to which I became addicted after it was strongly recommended by a favourite instructor. To this day, I never miss an issue, and recommend its eponymous style guide to the many talented young men and women who spend stints interning or working on my policy team.

The one other habit I picked up in my twenties was a fondness for audiobooks, read out either by the author or a professional narrator. It started with audiobooks on cassette tapes and compact discs, to downloadable digital content and, now, apps that handle it all with ease. Machine intelligence has also advanced to the level that computer readouts of e-books no longer sound like some dated sci-fi movie with talking robots, but quite human-like. It is to these technologies that I am grateful, for being able to 'read' a book every week, almost all non-fiction.

From early in my first term in the Rajya Sabha (in 2000), I started participating in television studio discussions (which, then, had far less of a 'fish market' ambience), policy-related conferences and foreign policy Track-II dialogues. It was often suggested to me that I ought to write op-ed columns and that I should approach people in that line of work. But, while I enjoyed writing as much as reading, I was uncomfortable reaching out to seek platforms to publish on.

I am grateful to Shekhar Gupta, then editor of *The Indian Express*, who, more than a dozen years ago, became the first newspaperman to ask me to write an op-ed. When I did so, he complimented my work and encouraged me to keep writing. From time to time, his team would reach out to me and I would write a piece on something of current interest that I had worked on in my day job.

Soon, others began noticing and asking me to write as well. Notable among them has been Swagato Ganguly of *The Times of India*, who first got me to write occasional pieces in the *Times*, and then to write a regular monthly column for the past four years. He has thoughtfully encouraged my attempts to delve deeper into controversial issues, exploring arguments and counterarguments from all sides, as well as having occasionally critiqued my work and given constructive feedback.

I am also grateful to have had the opportunity to write op-eds for *The Economist*, British Broadcasting Corporation (BBC) Online, and *The Wall Street Journal* among international publications; and in India, *Outlook, India Today, Hindustan Times, The Asian Age, Daily News and Analysis, Dainik Jagran, Sambad* and *The Samaja*, among others.

While the vast majority of these experiences has been wonderful, there have been occasional disappointments, such as the couple of times when I wrote something on request, only for it to not be carried. I also had a peculiar experience when a publication (not named here) carried my op-ed but edited out a sentence, not because of space constraints but because it pointed out an inconsistency in the stand of one of the editor's favourite political leaders. I disagree with wasting people's time, or 'editing' their opinions, and so have prioritized writing for those platforms that don't do that.

Though I envy some prolific columnists—a few of whom I have seen write coherently at great speed—my own style is much more deliberate and methodical. I draw upon ideas from both my life experiences as well as my reading. But when writing, I continually do web searches, to cross-check facts as well as delve deeper into an idea, thought or argument, as well as try to understand the best counters to it.

Each word of these articles has been written by me. But I have also been fortunate to have had a series of bright young men and women work on my policy team—a few full-time, but most on fellowships and internships. They have contributed to the significant research and fact-checking that goes into all my published writing, as well as into developing my positions on matters of policy in and out of the Parliament.

Though space does not permit me to mention all those who have helped me learn and grow, and provided me with the platforms to share my thoughts, I must mention a few. My high school English and history teacher, Mr Y.J.S. Ambrose, gently encouraged my writing. And in my adult life, Professor Jagdish Bhagwati and Lord Meghnad Desai—both people of great eminence, whom I admire—did me the great kindness of treating my views as worth listening to, discussing and debating. Their encouragement is something I cherish.

Finally, I must express my gratitude to Kapish Mehra of Rupa Publications, who was the first to ask me to write a book several years ago, and then he kept assiduously at it till the project came to fruition. In the process, he has also become a friend and, though he is several years younger, a philosopher and guide as well. I must also thank, and apologize to, a couple of other publishers who had also pursued me with vigour. I like and respect them, but ultimately felt most comfortable with Rupa.

I hope you enjoy reading these essays. And whether you agree or disagree, the most I seek from you, dear reader, is for you to recognize that these were the result of my honest efforts to understand and explain the issues of our times, shaped in the way I have been shaped—with curiosity and a willingness to speak candidly.

ONE

◆

OUR VIBRANT DEMOCRACY: PARLIAMENT AND GOVERNANCE

I had always considered myself reasonably well read and aware of the issues. And the activism that preceded my full-time involvement in politics had included much ranting about how politicians had messed up the country, which had led to friends telling me to either 'do something about it or stop whining'. But the lateral entry into politics in my thirties, after a dozen years in the private sector, came when I had already developed scepticism about 'the system'.

In my first few months as a member of parliament (MP), I kept getting surprised at how different many of my colleagues were in person, in comparison to their caricatured images in public. Many of them came across as far more thoughtful and knowledgeable in private, and something dawned on me.

It was that politicians, like people in any other walk of life, were also creatures of the environment within which they operated. And that their individual foibles, preferences and biases apart, the much stronger forces guiding their actions were systemic incentives and disincentives.

That got me to delve deeper into the history of how our parliamentary and political structures evolved, and how they compared with other countries, especially democracies. The more I read, discussed and argued, the more I became convinced that India has been carrying certain systemic legacy bottlenecks that we need to overcome.

Some of these legacy bottlenecks have to do with the parliamentary system prevailing in the United Kingdom (UK) in the late nineteenth century, on which much of our pre-independence proto-parliament was modeled. But the UK has moved on, as have legislatures in other respectable democracies.

One example is the balance of powers between two houses of parliament in a bicameral system. Ours is still plagued by systemic gridlock between the Lok Sabha and the Rajya Sabha. By contrast, in two significant reforms in the twentieth century, the UK took away its upper chamber's right to an absolute veto over the popularly elected house's legislation, leaving it with the power to only slow down the legislation it deems unwise, by up to a year, when either the popular mood would still hold or cooler heads would prevail.

Similarly, over the decades, our electoral system has evolved into having the world's lowest ratio of governance to campaigning. The Westminster model of democracy, which originated in a relatively small and homogenous nation, has taken on unexpected dimensions in our humongous and diverse nation, such as being continually in election mode.

Some colleagues have argued that India would be much better served by a presidential system of democracy. I inherently agree, but also believe that the odds of being able to build a national consensus around the idea is abysmally low. There is simply too much polarization in our polity, and the possibility of putting together another constituent assembly of eminent men and women whose integrity is respected across the political divide, is unthinkable today.

The more practical approach would be to address the problems that our current system throws up, with a series of fixes, which, done over a period, may be far more feasible. There are examples aplenty from other democracies, which we ought to study and consider for adapting to our requirements. But this, too, will require debate and consensus building, as well as overcoming resistance to change, which is sometimes rooted more in fear and suspicion than in rational considerations.

1

A SHORT HISTORY OF ELECTRONIC VOTING MACHINES

They are to paper ballots, what motor vehicles are to horse-drawn buggies

Alleging voter fraud through the tampering of electronic voting machines (EVMs) is a time-honoured tradition by losing candidates and parties in India. This tradition began from the very first instance of the use of EVMs, when the Election Commission (EC) tried out a pilot project during the Kerala assembly elections in 1982.

In fact, Communist Party of India candidate Sivan Pillai challenged the use of EVMs even before the election could be held, but the Kerala high court (HC) did not entertain him. However, the fun was only just beginning, since Pillai, despite his apprehensions, ended up winning. Thereupon, it was the turn of the losing Congress party to challenge the use of EVMs and Pillai's victory, setting in motion a practice that has since become de rigueur for any self-respecting loser of an election in Indian. Not all losing candidates go to court against EVMs, of course, but it has almost come to be considered bad form if the loser does not at least hold a press conference to denigrate them.

Ironically, in that first instance, the Congress actually prevailed. Though the HC had turned down its argument that the Representation of the People Act (RoPA), 1951, and Conduct of Election Rules, 1961, did not provide for EVMs, on appeal, the Supreme Court (SC) eventually ruled in its favour in 1984. In the resultant re-election conducted with traditional paper ballots, the Congress candidate beat Pillai. Although that, by itself, was no proof against the veracity of EVMs, it has remained a beacon of hope for election losers over the decades.

In any event, the 1984 SC ruling against EVMs had been on grounds of a legal technicality and not about their fundamental suitability. That flaw was corrected by a 1988 amendment to the RoPA, providing the legal framework for use of EVMs. In yet another historical ironic twist, this was passed by a Parliament dominated by the Congress, the only beneficiary of EVMs being set aside in favour of paper ballots.

The incorporation of machines, technology and automation in electoral voting goes back to at least 1892, when the first lever voting machine was used in New York, after decades of relying on paper ballots. Punch-card voting machines were introduced in the US in the '60s, and were still in use in Florida four decades later, when their malfunctioning helped make the 2000 presidential election controversial. The US also saw the first EVMs introduced in 1975.

Gloriously Entertaining Tradition

Automation helps improve the efficiency and speed of voting and counting. But it has been even more important in overcoming fraud and aiding the crucial democratic requirement of secret ballots, both aspects being much more vulnerable in manual voting. These, and the huge logistical challenges of paper ballots, were the reasons why India's EC pushed for EVMs, after widespread malpractices in the '70s.

Democracy in India has made much progress over the decades, with the rest of the world going from being cynical about its survival, to now treating it as a triumphant role model. At least since the era of T.N. Iyer Seshan* in the early '90s, the EC has arguably become our most respected institution, not to mention helping several other nations run their elections better. EVMs have played a significant

---

*T.N. Iyer Seshan was an IAS officer and chief election commissioner from 1990–96, who is remembered for reforming elections in India.

role in this transition, which has seen a drastic reduction in voting malpractices.

Those who demand a rollback to paper ballots are wrong, and forget why we moved on from them. After all, despite the real risks of road accidents, we don't abandon motor vehicles and go back to horse-drawn carriages. Instead, we implement safety measures like speed limits, seat belts and helmets. Of course, no technology is infallible, and credible allegations of EVM tampering must be taken seriously. Fortunately, the EC has done so. In 2009, it conducted the highly publicized exercise of asking petitioners to demonstrate tampering; none could. Similarly, the Delhi HC in 2004 and the Karnataka HC in 2005 had rejected petitions challenging EVMs, after examining the reports of scientific and technical experts.

In April 2017, in a case of an EVM allegedly yielding votes for only one party, the EC enquiry found that the allegation was untrue. Such quick responses to specific allegations, random audits and public demonstrations, by the EC, are essential to reinforce EVMs' reliability.

However, two aspects of EVMs in India, which remain work in progress, are important to improve the electoral system further. First, the EC's proposal to use 'totaliser' machines to aggregate the vote counting of multiple EVMs has been stymied by litigation as well as the government's disagreement. This relates to the core issue of secret ballots being crucial for democracy. Without this, voters at any particular booth run the risk of being victimized for not voting for powerful interests.

Finally, a new generation of EVMs was developed in 2011 with a feature for Voter Verifiable Paper Audit Trail. As the name implies, these make it vastly easier to audit and verify the votes cast, if challenged. After an SC judgment to deploy such EVMs by 2019, the EC has already commissioned 20,000 of them and is awaiting funding for the rest.

This would take EVMs' trustworthiness beyond reproach, but would sadly end a thirty-five-year-old gloriously entertaining tradition.

This article was first published in *The Times of India* on 12 April 2017

2

ONE NATION, TWO ELECTIONS

*How to stop parties from always being in
campaign mode and get them to govern*

There is much to be proud of regarding the democracy of India, which is not only the world's largest, but also its most diverse. Over the decades, we have disproved the many critics who doubted that India could remain democratic. But despite this success, our republic suffers from a worrisome shortcoming: too much campaigning, too little governance.

The continual cycle of elections—with several at the state level every year—inevitably impacts governance at the national level. Every such election is a significant distraction for the union government, since it is inevitably seen as at least a partial referendum on the government's policies and functioning.

This often leads to policy announcements being held up, lest they impact the outcome. And in frequently requiring senior members of the government to be off campaigning, it also acts as a drag on the bandwidth available for governance. Frequent elections impact Opposition parties as well, for similar reasons, thus repeatedly polarizing political discourse and reducing the room available for compromise.

For India to adequately grapple with its many challenges, the ratio between governing and campaigning must improve at both its national as well as state levels. Certainly, no other democracy has anything quite like this in terms of continual elections.

The first four general elections held in 1951–52, 1957, 1962 and 1967 saw largely simultaneous nationwide exercises for both the Parliament and the state assemblies. The only two exceptions were Kerala and Odisha, which had midterm elections in 1960 and 1961, respectively.

Thereafter, this broad alignment got further disrupted due to the frequent use of Article 356 of the Constitution (President's rule of a state) and also the use of Article 352 (emergency and extension of Lok Sabha's term by a year).

While SC judgments have narrowed the scope for the application of Article 356, there continue to be examples of its use, such as in Uttarakhand and Arunachal Pradesh, in recent years. Moreover, the lack of a clear mandate or the midterm collapse of both union and state governments have happened often enough to be another major cause of disrupting an aligned election cycle.

The disadvantages of misaligned, continual elections have been long understood, with many proposed solutions mooted over the years by credible individuals and institutions. These have included the Law Commission's recommendations from as far back as 1999, to more recent ones by a parliamentary standing committee and a white paper by the EC (not to mention exhortations by both the PM and the President).

Some of these proposals largely focus on a one-time reset. With this aim, they include a detailed consideration of how to overcome constitutional hurdles, such as extending or curtailing the ongoing terms of various state assemblies in order to synchronize all elections.

While that would indeed serve the immediate purpose, it would only buy time, due to the likely resurgence of misaligned elections. Even if, say, the use of Article 356 becomes passé, the odds are high that, over time, several state and national elections would yield fractured mandates and midterm elections.

However, the Parliamentary Standing Committee on Personnel, Public Grievances, Law and Justice, in its report in 2014, has suggested a two-cycle election process. Though all the election cycles would have the usual five-year terms, one would include polls for the Lok Sabha and about half the states, and the other cycle would be two and a half years later for the rest of the states.

Worth Taking Forward

The above mentioned elegant alignment would serve multiple objectives. First, it would do a better job of overcoming hurdles. For example, the EC's earlier idea of a one-cycle election, where a state with a fractured mandate would have a re-election only for the balance of its original five-year term, would likely generate resentment and objections. It would also be less cost-effective. A two-cycle system would simply align such a state's election to the next cycle, getting it closer to a full five-year term. And that would work just as well for the Lok Sabha, if needed.

Second, a two-cycle alignment of all state and national elections would serve a fundamental democratic purpose—that of rendering broad public opinion to the union government of the day. As mentioned above, this happens inefficiently today, with its continual distraction and even small, one-state elections creating disproportionate drag on governance.

The proposed alternative of a second election cycle would have voters from about half the country voicing their opinion at the midpoint of the union government's term. This would serve as an appropriately sized referendum, congealed together, rather than in distracting dribs and drabs. The US has a somewhat similar system (though their midterm cycle includes elections for some senators and states, and all Congressmen) and it often serves as a wake-up call to the federal government. Finally, a two-cycle election system would serve yet another aim of democracy—that of furthering a system of checks and balances in the polity. That, too, happens inefficiently today, stretched out over many individual elections.

Following the parliamentary standing committee report, the National Institution for Transforming India (NITI Aayog) has done a creditable job of going into the nitty-gritty of how such two-cycle elections could work. It is worth taking that forward.

The catchphrase 'one India, one election' has been gaining traction. In fact, India would be better served by 'one nation, two elections'.

This article was first published in *The Times of India* on 21 December 2016

3

LESS CHECK, MORE BALANCE

Reforms must reduce the Rajya Sabha's power to block the
popular mandate, which is unparalleled globally

In October 2015, Italy's upper house of parliament, the Senate, voted to drastically reduce its own powers, including the number of members and the power to block constitutional amendments and other key legislation. Though steps like a public referendum and a passage by the lower house remain, in all likelihood this heralds the end of a decades-long era of chaotic governance. This ought to interest us in India, accustomed as we are to our version of chaotic governance. However, when Finance Minister Arun Jaitley mooted a relook at the Rajya Sabha's powers in August that year, it led to a furore from many quarters. Those objections continue, but in an unthinking, dogmatic way. It is important—and high time—that the issue is examined dispassionately.

First, let us be clear that democracies are crucially dependent on checks and balances. Thus, there are very good reasons for having a bicameral legislature, with one house representing the popular will of the day, and the other, with a longer perspective, exercising restraint against a potentially hysterical mob mentality.

However, governance in India, like in Italy and other countries earlier, is caught in a logjam of far too many checks and not enough balance. Nowhere else in the world are there as many legislative checks against the popular mandate of the electorate. Joint sessions of the Parliament are no solution as they are impractical to convene frequently and cannot pass constitutional amendments. Futhermore, structuring major legislation as money bills, solely to bypass the Rajya Sabha, is undesirable.

Breaking the Legislative Gridlock

It is instructive to consider how other democracies deal with these issues. Take, for instance, the UK, on whose Westminster model of parliamentary democracy, our system is mostly based. Till a century ago, its House of Lords could reject all bills except money bills, just like our Rajya Sabha today. However, in 1911, the Brits amended this, reducing its powers from being able to block legislation, to only being able to delay it up to two years. Then, in 1949, the House of Lords' powers were further diluted, so that today, with minor exceptions, all it can do is delay legislation for up to a year.

To be sure, the House of Lords is an appointed—not elected—body, though there are moves to change that. This is an aspect which has much confused the present debate in India. Those frustrated by the Rajya Sabha's intransigence often assert that it is an unelected house of nominated members and should not exert so much power.

Of course, that is a popular misconception: only twelve of the 245 Rajya Sabha members are actually nominated; the others being elected, albeit indirectly from the state assemblies rather than directly from the public. But this is a crucial distinction that cries out for greater introspection and debate.

The reality is that the Rajya Sabha's indirect elections are, indeed, akin to party nominations. This has been reinforced in recent years by two significant developments. The anti-defection law, while doing away with the ills of horse-trading, has had the unintended consequence of making party whips all-encompassing. This, in conjunction with the 2003 amendment that did away with secret voting by the members of legislative assembly (MLAs) for Rajya Sabha candidates, has all but ensured that only party-nominated candidates win.

In theory, the Rajya Sabha is supposed to represent the interests of states as a whole, but in practice, what it represents are the interests of parties—in fact, of party leaderships. Other democracies have faced, and resolved, similar problems. The most striking example is the US Senate, which the Rajya Sabha resembles in its members' terms of six years, with one-third retiring every two years. Originally, the US Senate was also indirectly elected from state legislatures, just like the Rajya Sabha today. But in 1913, during the so-called Progressive Era in the US, which saw many political reforms, the constitution was amended to enable senators to be elected directly by the public of each state.

The effect was dramatic. It broke the hold of party bosses to nominate cronies with no alignment with public interest. Furthermore, by requiring candidates to seek a plurality of votes all across a state, instead of just cosying up to party bosses, it forced eventual winners to reject fringe concerns in favour of centrist, broad-based campaigns.

India needs to choose one of two paths to break its systemic legislative gridlock. Emulating the UK or Italy would leave the Rajya Sabha electoral process intact, but reduce its powers. It would still have the ability to slow down the passage of bills, to ensure that those who win elections don't ride roughshod over the losers. But it would no longer have the power to indefinitely block legislation, thus ensuring that those who lose elections don't have a veto either.

Pursuing the American example would leave the Rajya Sabha's veto powers intact, but make election to it direct—by the public. This would make its members' agendas much less insular and more broadly aligned with public interest.

For either to happen, it will require a sustained championing by political leaders, much like US President Theodore Roosevelt did a century ago, or Italian Prime Minister (PM) Matteo Renzi has in the past few years. As in such reforms elsewhere, this would need, and deserve, support from the Opposition too—at least from those who hope to govern someday.

This article was first published in *The Times of India* on 26 November 2015

4

CASH TO ALL CITIZENS

Universal Basic Income could actually
work better in India than in rich countries

The idea of Universal Basic Income (UBI)—that is, a standard minimum cash subsidy to all citizens—is gaining traction in policy circles around the world. While the 'welfare state' roots of this idea go back to the eighteenth century, new twenty-first-century technologies have rekindled the debate.

Though most of the discussion so far has been in high-income countries, several Indian economists have also started to study and comment on UBI. Of course, the rationale, objectives and resources available vary widely between developed and developing nations, but whether our instinct is to agree or disagree with such an idea, it is time Indian politicians began debating it.

The prospect of millions of jobs being eliminated by automation is very real. A 2017 Oxford University study 'estimates that 47 per cent of jobs in the US are "at risk" of being automated in the next twenty years.' Similarly, a 2015 Australian study had concluded that 40 per cent of that country's jobs are at risk of being eliminated by technology, perhaps as soon as 2025.

Other such studies have policymakers worried in high-income nations throughout Asia and Europe. The jobs at risk are not just blue-collar ones in manufacturing, but also white-collar jobs, as artificial intelligence (AI) breaks new frontiers. For instance, IBM's Watson AI system is already outperforming many human doctors in diagnosing cancer.

Developing nations should worry even more. Any casual

notion that India can somehow buck a seismic shift in global technology trends would be foolhardy. For those thinking that our cheaper labour is somehow immune, or at least more protected, against technological upheaval, there are rude shocks in store. The World Bank has estimated that automation threatens to eliminate a stunning 69 per cent of all jobs in India, 77 per cent in China and 85 per cent in Ethiopia.

Technologies like driverless vehicles will drastically disrupt transportation economics and the millions of jobs associated with it. While there is disagreement about how soon that might happen, there are several ongoing field trials, and billions of dollars backing them. The first commercial rollouts are claimed to start within this decade.

If the past is anything to go by, some Indian politicians' first instinct will be to try and prevent the adoption of such new technologies here, in the name of preventing job losses. But this isn't the '80s any more, when bank computerization could be put off for more than a decade due to pressure from the unions. Today, any restrictions on new technologies would likely buy much less time for the status quo, not to mention hurting India in a brutally competitive world.

Has the Idea Reached a Tipping Point?

Lest you think UBI is being touted only by utopian socialists without a clue about how the real world works, consider that this time around, it is also being championed by some in that bastion of capitalism—Silicon Valley. In fact, start-up incubator Y Combinator is going beyond advocacy, with a planned UBI pilot project in California.

That is not to say that the idea has reached a tipping point in the developed world. In June 2015, even the egalitarian Swiss decisively rejected a proposed constitutional amendment to initiate a UBI of $2,500 per month. Nevertheless, Finland is launching a trial programme, where several thousand citizens will receive an unconditional grant of $600 per month in lieu of their existing benefits.

Much of the debate on UBI revolves around its affordability and the effect it might have on people's motivation to work. There is disagreement about how to make the arithmetic work in developed, welfare-state economies that have a high burden of public expenditure that would need drastic cuts. *The Economist*, a leading fiscally conservative magazine, shares those doubts, but also reckons that UBI could eliminate the poverty trap without denting the incentive to work.

Interestingly, several eminent economists like Pranab Bardhan of the University of California, Vijay Joshi of Oxford University, and Maitreesh Ghatak of the London School of Economics have argued that the arithmetic of UBI's affordability would actually work better in a country like India.

The reason is simple. In developed countries, funding UBI while keeping total social sector expenditure within reasonable limits would require brutal cuts to existing programmes that benefit the poor, the disabled and so on. In India, however, existing social sector spending is grossly inefficient, corruption-ridden, misdirected towards the better-off, and thus, unable to achieve the stated objectives.

Redirecting that wasteful expenditure, as well as some corporate tax exemptions, towards UBI could well make it viable in India. This view is supported by research undertaken by the National Institute of Public Finance and Policy (NIPFP), an autonomous institute under the Ministry of Finance.

While the Indian economy has bounced back from its recent lows, it is also increasingly clear that an 8 per cent GDP growth rate today creates far fewer jobs than it did in earlier decades. But NIPFP's Sudipto Mundle echoes many economists who worry about political hurdles to UBI, since restructuring public finances to accommodate it would affect many powerful interest groups.

In the past, India missed many opportunities as other developing nations passed us by. Today, while the developed world is increasingly diffident, India is being celebrated as the fastest-growing large economy. That still won't be enough to meet our demographic challenges, unless we are ready to think out of the box.

This article was first published in *The Times of India* on 27 October 2016

5

CASH MAY YET BE KING

This is corroborated by the success of conditional cash transfer schemes in Latin America

For years, there has been a growing debate in India about replacing hugely inefficient subsidies with cash or vouchers transferred directly into the hands of the poor, who could then procure goods and services from the open market—for example, food, fuel and education. Many eminent economists support the concept and there are successful experiences from other countries; yet, the political will has been slow to gather steam. There are broadly three objections, either explicit or implicit—first, an underlying distrust of market mechanisms; second, doubts about the beneficiaries' ability to make good choices with the money that they will get; and third, the logistics of fair disbursement.

Even now, with India on the verge of becoming the world's fastest-growing large economy, it would be a mistake to underestimate the distrust of markets. Jawaharlal Nehru is reported to have told Jehangir Tata that he considered 'profit' to be a dirty word, even in the context of the public sector. Perhaps, it was his revulsion towards capitalism that moulded the country's attitudes, or perhaps he was only reflecting the mood of a young republic that had just shaken off a centuries-old colonial rule that had its roots in trade and commerce. In any event, even after two decades of economic liberalization, modern India continues to be ambivalent towards markets and market mechanisms.

That should not be surprising, considering the egregious examples of crony capitalism that this country has repeatedly thrown up. It is not just the gigantic national scams dominating the headlines that reinforce this suspicion, but also the many midsize scandals that routinely come to light at state and city levels. Most of all, it is the billions of little frauds—the daily profiteering by district and village-level crony capitalists—that add to the scepticism.

Free market mechanisms, like lowered entry barriers and increased competition, have contributed immensely to economic growth and consumer benefit. Think of the burgeoning millions of Indians who can now afford such things as scooters, cars, phones, air travel, etc. Yet, the average Indian citizen's experience of markets continues to be coloured by such examples as the crony contractor who builds bad village roads, the crony non-governmental organization (NGO) that skims off governmental spending, and indeed the crony public distribution system (PDS) dealer who cheats the poorest of people.

Improving Lives

Harnessing the power of markets for the public good will be crucial if India is to improve the lives at the bottom of the pyramid. There is no other way to do it efficiently, at an affordable cost. This is already well recognized and made more palatable by couching it in constructs like Public-Private Partnerships (PPPs), at least for large projects. However, it will take many success stories at the village level before the aam aadmi will trust the system. The irony is that while the government lags behind in helping create these successes, those who can afford it, are voting with their feet. One example is the success of private rural schools that are delivering far better results than their much better funded government alternatives.

The second concern—about the ability of the poor to make rational choices—is not merely a patronizing attitude from a feudal past. Massachusetts Institute of Technology (MIT) professors Abhijit Banerjee and Esther Duflo, two celebrated young economists who famously pioneered randomized field studies in their discipline, give examples of seemingly irrational choices made by the poor in their seminal book, *Poor Economics: A Radical Rethinking of the*

Way to Fight Global Poverty.

Their analysis shows these to be linked to lack of information, beliefs, procrastination and the toll taken by very demanding lives. However, they also conclude that these choices are dramatically impacted by even small incentives. This is corroborated by the success of conditional cash transfer schemes in Latin America, where the stipulations have included children's school enrolment and basic preventive healthcare. Moreover, Banerjee and Duflo have also demonstrated that even non-conditional cash transfers tend to generally improve outcomes. The lesson seems to be that various approaches need to be combined, including respecting some of the choices made by the poor as well as structuring incentive-based transfers.

Finally, there is the question of how to reliably disburse cash transfers. A quarter of a century ago, Rajiv Gandhi famously accused the notoriously leaky government machinery of gobbling up 85 per cent of the funds spent on poverty alleviation programmes, leaving only a paltry 15 per cent for the actual beneficiaries. Not much has changed since then. The solution is not to try and improve this machine that is further complicated by intertwined networks of political patronage, but to bypass it as far as possible.

Technology holds the promise of that possibility. This is the one area where significant progress is being made, both by way of governmental initiatives like the Unique Identification programme, as well as the stupendous penetration of cellular phones, which have set the stage for potentially ubiquitous banking access. Put together, they make for a revolutionary combination: an inexpensive delivery mechanism and, critically, relatively easy beneficiary audits.

There is no consensus yet on any of these issues: whether to have cash transfers at all (if yes, then whether through vouchers, conditional transfers or unconditional transfers), the mode of disbursement, and so on. However, for one significant clue, it is possible to dismiss all the chatter on this subject as premature.

The giveaway is that politicians are finally catching on to the potential of this issue. In the 2009 elections, at least two of them—Nara Chandrababu Naidu in Andhra Pradesh and Vasundhara Raje in Rajasthan—aggressively championed cash transfers. Next time around, it is highly likely that they will have plenty of company.

This article was first published in *The Indian Express* on 6 June 2011

6

DO RESERVATIONS HELP?

Through knee-jerk extensions of quotas, politicians
achieve the opposite of stated aims

The topic of reservations in education and government jobs is, arguably, the most contentious of India's myriad threads of public discourse. It has led to much violence and many agitations, court rulings and constitutional amendments. At the same time, however, its basic premise has also seen rare political unanimity. This is why the Constitution's 1950 provision to initially institute reservations for a decade has routinely been extended by the Parliament.

The argument, in 1950, that sections of India's citizenry, who had been disenfranchised for millennia, needed a leg up, was undoubtedly strong. Meanwhile, irrespective of reservations, in the intervening sixty-eight years, democracy, per se, has made significant corrections. Though historical injustices can never be erased and elements of prejudice against some groups can still be seen, there are also many signs of empowerment, not the least of which is political clout.

What is less clear is whether, and to what extent, reservations have helped. This is because the constitutional requirement, that the progress that reservations contributed to should be assessed before deciding whether they need to be renewed, has never been done. In fact, there is precious little that has been studied about the impact of reservations.

Among the few credible assessments, in 2013, *The Economist* reported that the proportion of Dalits at the highest levels of the civil services had increased from just 1.6 per cent in 1965 to 11.5 per cent by 2011—and even more at lower levels—compared to their 16 per cent share of the overall population. But it cautioned against 'an obsession' with making government service representative rather than capable, which 'makes it too hard to remove (the) dysfunctional or corrupt'.

The report also acknowledged a steady improvement in Dalit literacy and higher education, and noted that the reservations policy 'probably does help', but again pointed out that it is difficult to distinguish between how much was contributed by reservations, and how much by the building of more schools, midday meals, etc.

Similarly, a 2010 study on the impact of reserved electoral constituencies on poverty, by academics Aimee Chin and Nishith Prakash, found mixed results. They concluded that while Scheduled Tribes (STs) are concentrated around reserved constituencies and did indeed see a decline in poverty, there was no such link for Scheduled Castes (SCs).

Such nuances have been lost on politicians, who have, almost without exception, supported knee-jerk extensions of reservations. Even for supporters of the basic principle behind quotas (there are studies showing that certain castes and religions face institutionalized discrimination in hiring) to not want to assess or modify them in order to improve their impact, is odd.

Engage with its Intricacies

The Economist bluntly says that the focus of Indian lawmakers has not been to assess whether reservation helps, but to extend it to 'new blocks of voters'. Policy guru Pratap Bhanu Mehta goes even further, writing that the current system of reservations is 'not about equal opportunity, it is about distributing the spoils of state power strictly according to caste, thus perpetuating it'. In other words, he concludes that it achieves the opposite of its stated aim.

Politicians' one-track attitude towards reservations has left only the judiciary to engage with the many relevant questions that have arisen. But, though courts have stipulated certain restrictions in reservations, many of those have been quickly overturned by subsequent legislation. To give just one example, the 1992 SC judgment disallowing reservations in promotions, lest it erode merit, was overturned by the Parliament's 77th constitutional amendment in 1995.

One SC stipulation that still stands, however, is the 1962 judgment that limits reservations to fifty. The reasoning was that reservation is meant to be an exception to the general rule of equality, and an exception cannot be more than a rule. Nevertheless, several states continue to violate this limit. Similarly, the court itself does not always stand strictly on principle, for instance, ruling that the 'creamy layer' of the OBC (other backward class) category be denied reservations, but not those of the SCs/STs category.

It is in this context that the Patidar movement, led by twenty-two-year-old firebrand Hardik Patel, has grabbed national attention. This is only the latest in a long line of similar movements and personalities, including many former household names. All of them faced opprobrium and so does Patel.

Despite the Patidars's demand for reservations being scoffed at by many commentators and social scientists as unwarranted, their angst is very real. Job creation has been slow for years, not just in high-growth Gujarat but all of India. This is exposing the other side of our large population of the working-age youth—the so-called 'demographic dividend'—which could just as easily become a demographic nightmare.

According to academic Christophe Jaffrelot, 'The Patels may well be the victims of the neo-middle-class syndrome. Those who have not yet arrived, who are part of this aspiring class, and find it difficult to achieve their goals because jobs are scarce, education is expensive…buying a car is hard, to say nothing about a home.'

This agitation, however, has a twist that is unprecedented. So far, none of the earlier agitations had demanded scrapping all reservations if their group was not included. There is no widespread political support for ending reservations, but, perhaps for the first time, there are signs that some politicians may now be willing to discuss its limitations and engage with its intricacies.

This article was first published in *The Times of India* on 3 September 2015

7

CAN 'MODICARE' WORK?

Critics doubt its funding but a sharp, counterintuitive strategy may ensure funds

As far as election year budgets go, the last full-fledged one—in 2018, of the Narendra Modi government's first term—belied predictions of populist excess. Buzz had been building that in anticipation of uphill electoral battles, the PM would throw caution to the winds and dole out freebies to all and sundry.

That did not happen.

In fact, privately, many Opposition politicians are breathing a sigh of relief, believing that they have more of a fighting chance in the next elections in the absence of widespread governmental largesse. Time will tell if they are right or wrong, but the point to be noted is that such relief represents conventional wisdom.

This is not to say that the Budget lacks ambitious social and political goals. It is worth examining the unconventional approach it takes for that—namely the healthcare plan targeting nearly 40 per cent of the population. Dubbed as 'Modicare' by some, it has elicited a full range of reactions, from being called 'unworkable' to 'revolutionary'. It is still in the early days, and many details of the plan are awaited. Nevertheless, there is already enough information in the public domain about its broad contours for an initial assessment. No one questions the scale of its ambition, touted as the biggest healthcare plan in the world, but most critics allege that it is impractical and the funding allocated for it is woefully inadequate—but is it?

It might seem so at first glance, but a closer examination reveals an approach that might qualify as a sharp, counterintuitive strategy.

Twist in the Tale

To begin with, some pundits miscalculated the numbers immediately after the Budget, misreading the hospitalization entitlement of ₹5 lakh as if it were for 500 million beneficiaries. In reality, the entitlement is *per* family for 100 million families. The second grossly-off-the-mark punditry, at least on many TV panel discussions in the aftermath of the Budget, counted the total payout as if every family would avail of it in full. In reality, of course, not every family experiences hospitalization for one or more members every year. And those who do, will, on average, avail far less than the full ₹5 lakh. A third objection is that the ₹2,000 crore allocated for this plan in the Budget is a pittance. Later, it became clear that this represents 60 per cent of the expected insurance premiums, with the states expected to bear the balance of 40 per cent. However, critics allege that even then, the combined ₹3,333 crore would be far short of what is needed.

Are they right?

The answer is both, yes and no, but with a twist in the tale that has interesting ramifications, possibly indicating a shrewder political strategy than the opponents have figured out. Critics make two sub-arguments here: first, that the insurance premium would be many times the NITI Aayog's estimate of ₹1,000–1,200 per family; and second, that even if the NITI Aayog is right, the funding needed for the premiums would be ₹10,000–12,000 crore, not ₹3,333 crore. But most critics, even non-political ones, proffer only broad alternative guesses rather than detailed estimates. Moreover, many acknowledge that the sheer size of the plan, covering an unprecedented 500 million beneficiaries, implies significant cost reductions from existing rates that are not easy to estimate.

The NITI Aayog's estimate is likely correct, backed by detailed analysis and corroborated by Andhra Pradesh's existing Rajiv Aarogya Raksha plan, which costs ₹1,200 per individual for ₹2 lakh cover for more than 1,000 diseases. The much larger scale of 'Modicare' should see similar premiums per family, even for a higher cover.

The second argument, that even then—and even after including the states' contribution—the allotted funding adds up to only a portion of the required amount, is a more relevant issue. The answer to that must surely lie in the near certainty that not all states will hit the ground running in the first year. Since this plan is as much of a surprise to them as to anyone else, many states will need time to get their act together to figure out how much they can allocate and the nuts and bolts of the scheme. Of course, by next year, the funding allocation for Modicare in the Union Budget will need to be sharply increased.

There are other wrinkles to be ironed out as well, such as, where many of the beneficiaries will go for hospitalization, how smoothly (or not) the system will work, and so on. Recent years have seen several similar healthcare plans, albeit smaller, at both state and national level. They have had a mixed record, but one that encourages optimism. This is because of the surge in private medical facilities that can be harnessed by the government.

Finally, the use of technologies like Aadhaar are revolutionizing the delivery of services far more efficiently. It could well be that massively ambitious sociopolitical goals may no longer require the kind of massive boondoggles they used to.

In the meantime, the PM's party has an opportunity to rapidly roll out 'Modicare' in the states it runs. If it can demonstrate early success stories, it would be child's play for the master communicator to sell it to voters and to rub opponents' noses in it, in states that are slow off the mark.

This article was first published in *The Times of India* on 14 February 2018

8

A QUOTA FOR WOMEN

*This is one big idea awaiting implementation
by the Modi government*

For nearly a quarter of a century, every union government till the present one has unsuccessfully attempted to enact a women's reservation bill for quotas in the Parliament and state assemblies. The governments of PMs H.D. Deve Gowda (1996–97), Atal Bihari Vajpayee (1998–2004) and Manmohan Singh (2004–14) each introduced the bill once or more. Only the tenure of Inder Kumar Gujral (1997–98) did not see such an attempt, but that was essentially a continuation of the same United Front government that had already done so under Deve Gowda, with a change of PM. As the Modi government's first term enters its last lap, the issue is again gaining traction. Will he give it a shot as well? What are the bill's merits and, just as relevantly, what is its political viability?

Though reservations in India have had a mixed track record and continue to be a source of contentious politics, they have also played a role in challenging age-old social barriers. Nevertheless, pleas to modify reservations, such as limiting them to one generation of beneficiaries (thus, rigidly excluding the more affluent 'creamy layer' among them) and exclusion from highly technical disciplines, are all worthy of debate. But what is undeniable is that the status of women in India, who, as a category, far surpass the numbers of any other group facing discrimination, continues to lag well behind global norms. From the womb onwards, women still have it rough in the world's second-most populous nation. Despite anti-sex-selection laws and some improvement in recent years, the gender ratio remains skewed with fewer births of females than males.

Indian women's lives are burdened by low literacy (59 per cent versus a national average of 74 per cent), even lower levels of financial inclusion (42 per cent versus developed countries' averages approaching 100 per cent); and shockingly low participation in the workforce (only 28 per cent compared to even South Asian neighbour Bangladesh's 45 per cent). Similarly, the percentage of women elected to the Lok Sabha, at just under 12 per cent, is about half the global average of 23 per cent. However, the share of female legislators is not necessarily correlated to a nation's gender equity. Consider three examples from developed, Western democracies—the type of nations generally hailed for the relatively better, if not quite equal, status of women: the United States (US) has only 19 per cent women in its lower house; the UK, 30 per cent; and Sweden, 45 per cent. Sweden is the only one of those three nations with a law promoting women in politics, but by regulating parties rather than the parliament. Its 1971 law, when its share of women legislators was 14 per cent, stipulates a women's quota of 40 per cent of all party candidatures. This is an alternative that has also been mooted by some in India, with a 33 per cent quota of party tickets.

Transformational Impact

Quotas for women in state and national elections may not, by themselves, be a panacea for gender rights. In fact, starting from freedom fighter Sarojini Naidu, till today, several prominent women have spoken against them. Many activists also give equal or more emphasis to other building blocks of gender equity, especially to boost women's participation in the workforce. This approach is supported by studies that indicate a strong correlation between more working women and better gender equity.

Programmes like the 'Beti Bachao Beti Padhao' campaign championed by the PM, as well as a growing number of individual success stories, are also gradually stigmatizing discrimination. The latter include female fighter pilots, autorickshaw drivers, sporting stars, chief executive officers, entrepreneurs and many more. However, attitudinal changes in society take a long time. So, notwithstanding governmental programmes and individual successes, a sharp improvement in the medium term will require additional intervention.

Quotas for women in local body elections have been in place for years. Observing the impact of that on the ground is eye-opening. On the one hand, many a female sarpanch or Zilla Parishad member is just a rubber stamp, with a male relative wielding the real authority. On the other hand, I have witnessed several such elected women come into their own, handling the hurly-burly of politics themselves, and with aplomb. Such women are influencing others and changing societal attitudes.

This is why I believe quotas for women could be transformational for India's politics, society and economy, especially if the proposed sunset clause after fifteen years could actually be hardwired. Some sceptics worry that that would not be the case, as with other reservations, but even then, the impact of a higher number of women in the Parliament and the assemblies would have an overwhelmingly positive impact.

The above rationale apart, the political will for it has never been enough to overcome opposition. Furthermore, PM Modi has been seeking transformational change through mega persuasion campaigns instead of by legislation—for example, the exhortations of the 'Swachh Bharat' programme, rather than, say, emulating Singapore's harsh punishments for littering. Presumably, the PM's similar exhortations on gender equity could be construed as his preferred alternative to quotas.

But he is also known to spring surprises. And considering the potentially huge political benefits from co-opting a big women's issue, it should not be ruled out. Despite the fact that it is the United Progressive Alliance (UPA) chairperson Sonia Gandhi who has again spoken up for it, this government has a demonstrated track record of pushing through, and thus gaining credit for, big ideas that had been gridlocked for decades.

This article was first published in *The Times of India* on 14 March 2018

9

TRANSFORM, DON'T TINKER

*India is undergoing steep educational
decline that must be reversed*

It was a made-for-TV moment, waiting to happen for years. In 2016, when an enterprising journalist cruelly exposed two 'toppers' of the Bihar Class XII board exams by asking them basic questions, to which they gave embarrassingly clueless answers, no one should have been surprised; for, all the precursors necessary to lead up to this pathetic situation have been on full display for years.

Who can forget the annual scenes of hordes of exam-takers' relatives clambering up several outer walls in order to hand cheat sheets to their wards? And though most egregious in Bihar, it is far from being the only state where that happens. It is no small mercy that the state's education minister responded not with brazenness, which has become evermore common, but with some contrition and the announcement of a partial re-examination.

The decline has been evident from India's appalling education statistics, not to mention the government's responses to them. The most infamous of these, the Program for International Student Assessment (PISA) debacle, is, by now, fairly widely known. After India ranked #73 out of seventy-four participating countries in the 2009 round of the PISA, the Ministry of Human Resource Development pulled out of any further participation in it.

The excuse given then was that since PISA was conducted by the Organisation of Economic Co-operation and Development (OECD), a group of developed nations, there was a sociocultural disconnect between the questions and Indian students. But that hardly explains the better performance by students of non-OECD countries who participate in PISA, such as Vietnam, Thailand, Malaysia, the United Arab Emirates, Uruguay, Tunisia, Jordan and Kazakhstan.

As should be expected, the PISA scores were not an isolated example. Year after year, credible domestic and international stakeholders expose India's alarming education scenario, the United Nations (UN) Educational, Scientific and Cultural Organization's 2012 Education for All Development Index ranked India #102 out of 120 countries. And the well-regarded Pratham, an NGO, in its 2014 Annual Status of Education Report, concluded that 60 per cent of Class III students cannot read a Class I text, and 74 per cent of Class V students cannot do division.

In this gloomy scenario, it is only fair to recognize the improvements that have been. In the past fifteen years, the Sarva Shiksha Abhiyan programme has seen dramatic improvements in the infrastructure of government primary schools. There has been a sea change in the form of an increase in the number of school buildings, classrooms and even toilets. But significant inadequacies remain, especially at the secondary level, such as the paucity of science labs in many a school.

Challenges Galore

In any event, the brick-and-mortar part of education is necessary, but not sufficient, to deliver results. There are many other challenges to be overcome, not the least of which is teacher absenteeism. A World Bank study concluded that one out of every four teachers is usually absent in India, and only half were teaching. Proposed solutions include daily cash incentives for teachers and attendance monitoring with cameras, while others have said teachers are already well paid but need better work conditions.

The 2009 Right to Education Act (RTE), enacted in the middle of a decade devoted to rights legislations, was well intentioned. Its champions believed that making education every child's right would transform the sector in much the same way that the 2005

Right to Information Act (RTI) galvanized activism. The reality has been markedly different.

Some of the RTE's utopian ideas have already fallen victim to the law of unintended consequences, such as the estimated 8,000 private schools that shut down according to Geeta Kingdon, an educationist at the London University. While the intention was to impose minimum infrastructure standards on potentially fly-by-night schools, the result has often been to penalize the many poorly equipped private schools that have nevertheless been producing far better results than their well-funded government counterparts.

The RTE provision to no longer hold back underperforming students for an extra year is opposed by many on the grounds that it is a cynical way to keep enrolment numbers high, while contributing to the atrocious exam results. A section of RTE opponents are also exercised by the exemptions provided to minority institutions, which they perceive as unfair and harmful to national consensus building. However, there seems to be little governmental appetite to reconsider that, especially since a five-judge SC constitutional bench has upheld it.

Nevertheless, much is sought to be addressed by a new National Education Policy, though that itself is facing its own share of controversy. The kerfuffle about the right time to release a report commissioned by the government—whether immediately, or after the states have commented on it—is a storm in a teacup. The issue of far more concern should have been the reason as to why it was given to mostly retired bureaucrats, rather than academics and experts, to prepare.

Despite all this, it is heartening to see increasing examples of bright students emerging from rural areas—some from government schools, but proportionately many more from schools run by missionaries such as the Saraswati Shishu Mandirs, which are now matching the traditionally successful convent schools, as well as NGOs, and even low-cost, for-profit schools. All these need to be encouraged, not hindered.

The big challenge remains the adequate funding of education, while keeping it free of the red tape that is stifling it. It remains to be seen if this government is looking to tinker or transform.

This article was first published in *The Times of India* on 8 June 2016

10

GIVE IT UP

Members of Parliament don't need
subsidized snacks to do their job

In 2015, about a million Indians relinquished their liquid petroleum gas (LPG) subsidies in less than four months since PM Modi urged them to 'Give It Up' voluntarily for the benefit of the more disadvantaged sections of society. Many middle-class households have let go of the subsidy, which should ideally prioritize the poorest of the poor (Below Poverty Line [BPL] households) as well as those rural households that are currently using inefficient and harmful cooking fuels. As of now, the benefits of the LPG subsidy are skewed in favour of a few large industrialized states (Maharashtra, Andhra Pradesh, Tamil Nadu, Uttar Pradesh and Karnataka corner 50 per cent of this subsidy) and that too in wealthy households in primarily urban areas (about 60 per cent). Less than 15 per cent of rural households use LPG as their primary cooking fuel and, instead, rely largely on firewood.

If a million Indian citizens can give up subsidized LPG cooking fuel connections, then surely a few hundred MPs can also give up subsidized food at the Parliament canteen. Government subsidies are meant for those who cannot afford to pay the full price of a service or product. Surely, MPs can offer to give up this subsidy (or a VVIP privilege, if you will) to set right this anomaly. Not just that, if we do the right thing—by appropriately targeting subsidies in this case, and not carrying on with a sense of VVIP entitlement—it will be a step towards effecting greater public trust and confidence in our role as lawmakers.

I gave up my gas subsidy some years ago. Over the years, I have also been advocating the dismantling of the well-entrenched VVIP culture in India, ranging from topics relating to red light beacons, security frisking, toll collection on highways, etc.

Central Principles

While the quantum of the Parliament canteen food subsidy might not be huge, the central principles that need consideration are:

- Redirecting of subsidies to those who need it the most.
- Implementing the subsidy transfer efficiently, by fixing leakages and eliminating any scope for corruption.

In the case of LPG, the 'Give It Up' campaign relates to the former point, by nudging the citizenry to give up the gas subsidy so as to enable it to be more widely accessible to the poorest of the poor. The Direct Benefits Transfer for LPG (DBTL) programme is an attempt at operationalizing the latter point, whereby the subsidy is directly affected through cash transfers into bank accounts, which virtually eliminates any scope for leakage and corruption. (However, it needs to be noted that as yet, the DBTL programme has not been a targeted cash transfer scheme.) Ideally, the net impact of the above two principles is that the subsidy net gets cast widely as well as efficiently to those that really need it, thus ensuring a bigger impact of government spending on social sector schemes.

Some people have pointed out that the beneficiaries of the subsidized canteen food are not only MPs, but also the staff working in the Parliament. However, government employees are most likely not to fall in the category of the poorest of the poor for whom government subsidies are usually intended, and can most probably afford to forego the subsidized food. As a response to the 'Give It Up' campaign, government employees have also been surrendering their subsidized LPG connections. However, if there is indeed a strong case for them to keep availing of the subsidized food facility, the model that needs to be emulated is the DBTL programme, which ensures a transparent and direct transfer of benefits. Like in the case of the DBTL programme, the government employees who use the Parliament canteen can get direct cash transfer as a perk or subsidy.

MPs can certainly afford to go without subsidized food and continue to conduct legislative business in the Parliament. But where they *do* need support is by way of provision of an office, trained staff and other resources, which will help them to go about their work efficiently.

This article was first published in *HuffPost* on 20 July 2015

11

SAVING THE LEGISLATIVE SETUP

Delay in session shows why poll reforms are vital

After a prolonged hue and cry, and threats of being nullified, the Parliament's Winter Session began from 15 December 2017, and went on till 5 January 2018. India's Parliament holds three sessions every year. The Budget Session, being the longest one, is held towards the beginning of the year, then the Monsoon Session in July–August, and finally, the Winter Session in November–December. Constitutionally, Article 85 only mandates that there should not be a gap of more than six months between any two parliamentary sessions. Usually the Winter Sessions begin in November and are held till December each year, but in 2003, 2008 and 2013, due to elections in the states of Chhattisgarh, Madhya Pradesh, Rajasthan, Delhi and Mizoram, the session did not begin in November but only after the last polling day. In 2008, even though the Winter Session started early in October, it was halted between 24 October and 9 December due to elections. The National Democratic Alliance was in government in 2003, while in both, 2008 and 2013, it was the UPA.

This disparity in parliamentary proceedings can be attributed to state elections. It is, therefore, necessary to improve the ratio between governance and campaigning at both the national and state levels. Parliamentary sessions will be inevitably delayed unless reforms in both the electoral schedule and the Lok Sabha are implemented. The constant juggling of roles in politicians' lives renders them unable to perform their duties and obligations in a cogent manner. The finance minister's statement, that the government would ensure a regular Winter Session but would not want it to clash with the

9–18 December Gujarat Assembly elections is a testimony to the fact that ceaseless election cycles in our country cause havoc in governance. The 2017 Gujarat Assembly elections saw senior leaders of major political parties engrossed in it, leaving them unable to perform many vital constitutional duties. Continual elections are not only a distraction from governance but also prevent the Opposition parties from effectively playing their role in the Parliament. This continuum adds to uncertainty in parliamentary proceedings, leading to delays in matters of urgency.

The functioning of the country is impacted by the functioning of its legislature. A declining trend has been observed in the sitting days of the Parliament. The Lok Sabha met for an average of 130 days in a year during the 1950s, and these were further reduced to seventy days in the 2000s. The National Commission to Review the Working of the Constitution recommended that the Lok Sabha should have 120 sittings in a year, and the Rajya Sabha should have a hundred sittings, but despite that, this year we will have the shortest Winter Session in twenty years.

There is no fixed legislative calendar in place for India, unlike in Canada, the US and the UK, where parliaments are in session throughout the year. In these countries, every year begins with the formalization of a sittings calendar, and other legislative allied businesses are programmed accordingly. In 1955, similar efforts were tried in India too, with the Lok Sabha recommending a calendar of sittings—but in vain. Having the Parliament sit on known dates would enable proper planning and policy work. Some state legislative assemblies have tried addressing this disparity by specifying a minimum number of working days in their procedural rules. The Odisha Assembly has a mandatory provision specifying the number of days it would meet. Uttar Pradesh, too, has a provision to ensure best efforts for working out meetings for a specified number of days.

There seems to be a growing consensus within the country on holding simultaneous elections. These include credible institutions and individuals. After the 1999 Law Commission recommendation and the parliamentary standing committee report on simultaneous elections, the NITI Aayog has suggested that for the purpose of easing the political and technical issues of holding simultaneous elections in one go, these could be considered in two phases. Thus, Phase 1 could be in sync with the 2019 Lok Sabha polls—in April to May 2019; while Phase 2 could be held midway in the new Lok Sabha's term, approximately thirty months after Phase 1—say, around October to November 2021.

The idea of 'one nation, two elections', with state elections bunched around either the national election or a midterm cycle, would tackle many hurdles in an efficient manner. It would be cost-effective, avoid interruption in the delivery of essential services, and would, nevertheless, provide broad public opinion to the Central government of the day, without unnecessary distractions attributed to state elections. It will also enable improvement in India's abysmally low ratio of governance and campaigning due to ceaseless elections.

Globally, a similar structure can be observed in South Africa, with national and provincial elections held simultaneously for five years and municipal elections held two years later. Sweden, too, holds elections to its national legislature, provincial legislatures and municipal bodies on a fixed day—the second Sunday in September—for four years (the last one took place on 14 September 2014, and the forthcoming one is due on 9 September 2018.) The US, too, has a two-cycle election calendar, much like what has been mentioned above.

The issue of continual elections and the lack of a legislative calendar are ample justification for reforming the Lok Sabha and electoral rules. Other contentious matters, such as the legislative agenda being determined by a consensus in the business advisory committee, which is not transparent, the lack of number-based rules for initiating motions and the paucity of time that MPs face for preparation (that is, gaps between the notice of legislative agenda, circulation of papers and debate)—all need immediate ratification. Private members' bills are denied adequate time and, by convention, have not been passed since the early '70s.

These ailments need a cure, sooner rather than later, in order to save the legislative setup of our country and to reaffirm the belief and conviction of citizens in our vibrant democracy and its efficacy between elections.

This article was first published in *The Asian Age* on 18 December 2017

12

WHAT MODI CAN DO NEXT

The government looks unassailable now; bold policy moves to transform India must be undertaken

R are is the government that is stronger at nearly two-third into its term, than at the start. Yet, few would deny that that is the case with the Modi government, especially after the coup in Bihar in 2017, when it brought the redoubtable Nitish Kumar back to its fold. By most accounts, this has dealt a body blow to the Opposition. What are the implications of this for governance and reform? Not many would bet on this PM playing it safe from the current high till the next general elections.

That just does not seem to be his style.

There are already substantial changes underway. The Goods and Services Tax (GST) is beginning to drag large chunks of the informal economy into the formal one. The increasing use of Aadhaar and its unparalleled ability to 'deduplicate' beneficiaries, is drastically fixing the leakages in governmental schemes. India is finally getting international acknowledgement for its surge in infrastructure. And, going by the NITI Aayog and International Monetary Fund's (IMF) estimates, the Gross Domestic Product (GDP) growth rate again leads the world's large economies. However, the same growth rate today (for argument's sake, let's take the IMF's projected 7.2 per cent and 7.7 per cent for the next two years) no longer creates the same number of jobs it would have, a decade or two ago. The nature of the world's economies has changed, with far more automation and disintermediation than ever before. This remains a fundamental challenge for India.

Besides the above, UBI is an idea that is being championed

by many across the world, with a closely watched pilot project in Finland. While the debate on UBI is hotting up in India, it remains a cutting-edge but still untested idea, which deserves encouragement but also critical assessment, including randomized controlled trials.

Urgent Reforms

Meanwhile, there remain many conventional policy options to dramatically boost India's economy and governance standards. In some ways, these are 'no-brainers', tried and tested the world over, and brimming with common sense. Consider just three such reform options. Judicial (including an overhaul of the criminal justice system), administrative and labour are arguably the three most impactful areas in which restructuring would transform India's fortunes. In fact, they have all been attempted before, but lacked the political consensus needed to succeed. With the government's commanding position today, if the key members are persuaded of their utility, consensus will be less of a hurdle.

No society can function well if justice is uncertain or delayed. India's abysmally clogged judicial system, where even heinous crimes can take decades to investigate, prosecute and try, is in desperate need of reform. Besides our judicial system's woeful impact on social justice, poor contract enforceability is one of the biggest shackles on our economy. The last attempted judicial reform ended with the SC's tragic 2015 overthrow of the National Judicial Appointments Commission (NJAC), preserving the world's only self-appointing collegium system. NJAC had been based on UK's pathbreaking act, incorporating transparency and a system of checks and balances, and had unanimous political backing. With that unanimity now lacking, it is unlikely that this government will expend political capital on revamping judges' appointments. Nevertheless, opportunities abound in police, prosecutorial and judicial procedures' reform. But in the case of some of these, like funding an increased hiring for the police force, there are large cost implications whose benefits take a long time to show up and are not exactly ideal for election cycles.

Similarly, the creaky 'steel frame' civil service, designed in the nineteenth century for colonial aims, is at odds with twenty-first-century India's needs and aspirations. Sure, the service has bright people who pipped millions of others in an exam, but its systemic flaws, including generalists handling specialized domains, job security despite non-performance, short tenures at each post, and promotions on seniority rather than merit have long been a crippling choke point for the nation. Earlier PMs, including Vajpayee and Manmohan Singh, had attempted major administrative reforms but were forced to back down. However, the current PM seems to be going about it incrementally, and quietly. The government has started penalizing non-performers, and in 2017, modernized bureaucrats' appraisal system, including—for the first time—peers' and subordinates' feedback. There have also been reports of a significantly larger share of posts usually 'reserved' for the premier Indian Administrative Service (IAS) now going to allied service officers. Could this be a precursor to a lateral entry from outside the bureaucracy, which has been repeatedly recommended by experts? If yes, that would be excellent.

Finally, our counterproductive labour laws act as a massive brake on job creation, especially in manufacturing that has stagnated at around 16 per cent of GDP for more than three decades. Economists Jagdish Bhagwati and Arvind Panagariya have written that it is impossible to comply with all of India's approximately 200 labour laws. Even though the Union government as well as a few states have started tinkering with these laws, for the magnitude of job crisis that India faces, this is too little. A radical national level reform is required to significantly boost job creation.

Traditionally, all Indian political parties have relied on unions, making labour reform unachievable. However, Modi pushed GST through, despite apprehensions among his party's traditional base of small traders. With his government now looking unassailable, could lightning strike twice?

This article was first published in *The Times of India* on 2 August 2017

13

TOWARDS AN EMPOWERED RAJYA SABHA

Why we should put the House on steroids

The Rajya Sabha is often referred to by its erroneous nickname, the House of Elders—perhaps in deference to the UK's House of Lords, after which it was partially modelled. Its constitutionally correct nomenclature is, in fact, the Council of States, and reflects the other side of its roots, the US Senate. That seemingly minor difference hides an enormous chasm, reflecting fundamentally different objectives. This ambiguity about its raison d'être has always existed, but has grown over the years and now reached a crescendo.

In 2010, Madhya Pradesh Chief Minister (CM) Shivraj Singh Chouhan was reported to have said that the Rajya Sabha had become a market and should be abolished. His subsequently reported retraction could be due to political compulsions, but the comment touched a nerve, coming at the end of the derailed Winter Session of the Parliament that year, and deserves serious contemplation. He is right about some of the shortcomings of the Rajya Sabha, but wrong about the conclusion; throwing out the baby with the bathwater has never been a practical or desirable solution.

Though our system of democracy is largely based on the UK's Westminster parliamentary model, the Rajya Sabha is a curious blend of that country's House of Lords and the US Senate. Like the former, neither does it have the authority to amend money bills, nor is it required for the basic objective of providing a majority for government formation. Also, like the latter, it represents the states of the union, rather than individual constituencies, and has a rolling permanency, with one-third of its members elected every two years, which is not subject to the possibility of dissolution or midterm elections. Dr Bhimrao Ramji Ambedkar and his colleagues did a brilliant job of incorporating the best aspects of different political systems into our own Constitution, but stopped short of truly empowering the Rajya Sabha. Several of its original objectives have fared poorly over the years. The rolling permanency and indirect elections from the state assemblies, instead of the general public, were intended to provide a bulwark against extreme populism, but that role has got diluted and is now just as populist as the Lok Sabha. The related objective of providing an entry to eminent but unelectable personalities has also been partially thwarted, with the majority of its members now being hardcore politicians, and some of the others exemplifying the ills that Chouhan highlighted. However, we need to pause and wonder why we should have unelectable people as lawmakers anyway.

Evolving in the Opposite Direction

It's a legacy of colonial—even feudal—times, when the citizenry had to be given the vote but still could not be trusted with a full set of keys to the house. This may sound counterintuitive, but the true safeguard against extreme populism is not *less* democracy, but *more*—specifically, a system engineered to reward lawmakers (at least some of them)—and the Rajya Sabha is ideal for these to seek out centrist positions, rather than extreme ones. For that to happen, the Rajya Sabha needs to evolve in the direction opposite to the one it has been going in, in recent years.

In the past decade, amendments passed by the Parliament replaced the secret ballot for elections to the Rajya Sabha, with an open ballot, subject to party whips, and removed the state residency requirement for candidates, thus, fundamentally altering its character. Besides diluting its essence of representing states' interests in New Delhi, the Rajya Sabha membership has essentially become a party nomination rather than an election—even an indirect one. Almost without exception, the Rajya Sabha members are now mostly party apparatchiks or even a few outsiders, but in any case, subject only to the approval of party leaderships rather than even a rudimentary election. There are exceptions, of course, when parties, varying strengths in state assemblies, leave the odd Rajya Sabha seat up for grabs, but they are rare and are tailor-made only for tycoons with a penchant for politics.

Contrast that with the way the US Senate has evolved. While it, too, was originally elected from state legislatures, since the 17th Amendment to the US constitution in 1914, it has been directly elected by popular vote. Why was that amendment felt to be necessary? Political analyst Raffaela Wakeman has written:

> The senatorial election procedures from before the passage of the 17th Amendment…lacked many features that are now associated with desirable democratic practice. In particular, the identities of viable US Senate candidates were often obscured until the eve of the election in the state legislatures…with the winner often emerging through backroom deals…giving frequent victory to Senate candidates who would have been incapable of winning a popular election in the states they represented.

The striking similarities between elections to our Rajya Sabha today and those to the pre-1914 US Senate are obvious.

We desperately need an Indian equivalent of the US's 17th Amendment. The consequent direct elections and equally importantly, the large state-wide constituencies, will push candidates towards greater moderation and statesmanship.

Successful candidates will need to straddle the middle ground, instead of either just toeing party diktats or catering to the fringe. Such an empowered Rajya Sabha would be like an athlete on legally sanctioned steroids. Its greater capabilities would need to be matched with greater responsibilities, as in the US Senate, whose ratification is needed in key areas like foreign treaties and appointments to constitutional positions. Ironically, if corroboration is needed that the Rajya Sabha needs to become more like the American Senate than the British Lords, the latter is itself headed in the same direction. A Lords reform has been gathering steam in the UK for years and is on the verge of a major breakthrough.

This article was first published in *The Indian Express* on 17 December 2010

14

RESTORING THE HOUSE

How can the many obsolete rules and
conventions of the Indian Parliament be addressed?

As the depressingly familiar routine of parliamentary logjam plays out yet again, it is worth examining if the rising crescendo of criticism is nearing a tipping point that will finally tilt the balance in favour of a correction. However, the reality is that there will be no correction until the root causes—and not just the superficial symptoms—are addressed.

Both the criticisms and the proposed solutions, so far, treat parliamentary disruptions as the disease, whereas they are merely the symptoms. Notwithstanding a few younger MPs seemingly defying their leaderships with a 'no work, no pay' proposal (which, incidentally, I support, but only as a symbolic gesture), there has not been a serious debate on the root causes.

India's Parliament contains many obsolete rules and conventions that desperately need changing, without which it would be illogical to expect lasting change in its functioning (or lack thereof). These rules are rooted in the restrictions of the Raj-era limited democracy, as well as an earlier, more genteel era when Victorian norms, not rules, governed the settlement of disputes. In other words, they are not built to tackle the conflicts that, currently, we, as a nation, must work through.

First, the 'Raj hangover': well before Independence in 1947, the British gradually started involving Indians in governing India. A series of reforms, such as the Indian Councils Act of 1909, and the Government of India Acts of 1919 and 1935 gave Indians limited participation. Although elections were introduced, the ensuing elected body fell far short of being a parliament, with authority denied to it in many crucial areas. The idea was to devolve just enough power to keep the natives from rebelling, but mostly just to provide them a platform to blow off steam.

That mindset survives, with successive governments—and not just this one—happy to treat the Parliament as a platform for the Opposition to vent its ire, but not to the extent that it can exert true pressure. That would be too uncomfortable, requiring the government to mobilize its members, utilize its political capital and sell its agenda to the nation. Instead, every government strongly prefers the easy option of treating the Parliament as a toothless debating house, listening to the Opposition with an indulgent smile, and then doing exactly as it pleases. This is very 'British Raj'—except that we get to take turns being in charge!

This attitude, and the obsolete parliamentary rules which enable it, are at the heart of the problem. This is precisely why the government is loath to agree to debates that require voting (which is rather odd, considering that we are a democracy after all), since that would require of it all the above-mentioned labours for the passage of contentious proposals.

Precise Traffic Rules

This is where that other relic of the past accentuates the problem: the lack of precise rules and dependence on gentlemanly codes for settling disputes. With the exception of a no-confidence motion (the nuclear option threatening the very existence of a government), every other voting motion in the Parliament is left to the discretion of the Speaker—that is, to a consensus between the parties. That provides a veto to every side, making it totally unworkable.

An analogy would be the early days of automobiles, when there were so few of them that no hard and fast traffic rules were needed; if two happened to be at the same junction at the same time, both drivers could be counted on to arrive at a genteel and courteous solution as to who would go first. Today, that just would not work; without traffic lights and roundabouts, there would be utter chaos.

Indian democracy has come a long way in these seventy-two years; it has empowered millions of the previously disenfranchised, and it has become far more competitive. In line with this, its highest legislative body now needs precise traffic rules to function efficiently. What might these rules be?

To begin with, an attitudinal change can and should be facilitated by doing away with the paternalistic relics of Raj-era limited democracy. One example is that of private members' bills. By convention, these are never passed by the Parliament, acting only as moral suasion on the government. In fact, even to introduce such a bill, an MP needs to seek the President's permission! No such permission should be needed, and the convention of not passing them should be turned on its head. When it becomes normal for MPs, and not just governments, to author bills that become law, parliamentary participation will prove far more attractive.

Another example of paternalism is that, even after the Parliament passes a law, the government has the discretion of delaying its notification—that is, its implementation. That should go; any law passed by the Parliament should automatically become the law.

Most importantly, voting motions should be commonplace in the Parliament, as is the practice in most evolved democracies. Governments routinely reject Opposition demands for voting motions, with the taunt that they would entertain only the mother of all voting motions—the motion of no-confidence. That is a non-starter, since the Opposition will almost never have the numbers for it. Moreover, why should there be only two extreme alternatives of either a toothless debate or a no-confidence motion? There is plenty of room in the middle for voting debates that keep the government on its toes without jeopardising its continuance.

But safeguards are needed to prevent the Opposition from using flimsy excuses to punch above their weight. The best way to balance both is to do away with consensus and discretionary powers to decide what should be a voting motion. Instead, replace those with a precise rule requiring a demand from a substantial minority of MPs, say 33 per cent. If one of every three MPs asks for a voting motion, there ought to be one.

This article was first published in *The Indian Express* on 6 December 2011

TWO

POLITICS:
NO MORE PLATITUDES AND
POLITICAL CORRECTNESS

I ndian politics has, over the years, come to accept as 'normal' many practices that would shock the founding fathers and mothers of the republic. The overwhelming reliance on illicit 'black' money for campaigning, the prevalence of dynasties at both national and regional levels, the overt and direct political roles of many who face serious criminal charges, and other such abominations are among these.

So common have these become, that the majority of our elected representatives can no longer even conceive of a system without such distortions, or, at least, cannot believe that doing away with them is practical. Sadly, even the few who believe that reform can and must happen, have mostly just paid lip service to it. Few in public life have given much thought towards how to bring about such reform, let alone delved into the nitty-gritty of the systemic changes that are required.

For instance, it is one thing to say that criminal charges against elected representatives must be adjudicated swiftly (something which I support), but that needs two follow-up actions. First, it needs justification against the pushback that all citizens deserve justice at equal speed. The answer to this is that fast track courts already exist for specified objectives, and that this objective of eradicating criminality among lawmakers is an overwhelming necessity for the public good. And second, there must be a commitment to allocating the significant funds and resources that these solutions require.

Similarly, discussions on cleaning up political funding require facing up to certain brutal realities—for instance, the fact that our decades-long effort to cap campaign expenditures has not worked and has simply pushed political funding under the carpet and beyond scrutiny. There are good reasons to take a dramatically different approach—one that focuses not on the amount spent, but on their legitimacy and traceability. Another related and key objective—of providing a level playing field—can be better served by introducing state funding, that too in a manner that leverages small, legitimate and traceable political contributions.

There is an old adage about the difficulty that a fish has in comprehending the meaning of water, since that is what it is totally surrounded by, and cannot conceptualize anything beyond it. It is very similar to the acceptance that has settled down upon our polity. The way out of it is rather simple, because, unlike fish, we do have the ability to look beyond our 'water'.

There are plenty of analogies between different human experiences in societies around the world that we could gain from, by understanding and assessing them. All it requires is the desire and the acknowledgement that we can learn from others' experiences, especially those democracies that have faced near-identical issues over the centuries. Not all their challenges and solutions will be applicable to India, but some will, and others may yield new ideas for adapting to our circumstances.

1

TAKING CRIMINALS OUT OF POLITICS

Criminalization of politics does more than just subvert ethics in governance; it hits at the root of public engagement with the system

Today, the criminalization of politics in India is a sad reality. According to the Association for Democratic Reforms, seventy-six of the 543 members elected to the Lok Sabha in 2009 had been charged with serious criminal offences such as murder, rape and dacoity.

Under the present setup, getting elected to the legislature becomes a convenient shield to delay and extend the legal processes and escape conviction. The Second Administrative Reforms Commission noted that the 'opportunity to influence crime investigations and to convert the policemen from being potential adversaries to allies is the irresistible magnet drawing criminals to politics'.

Surprisingly, the current law goes overboard in offering protection to those convicted of criminal offences. Section 8(4) of RoPA allows an MP or MLA to retain his/her seat in the House even when convicted, if he/she files an appeal or an application for revision within three months from the date of conviction.

This section defies the ideas of equality enshrined in Article 14 of the Indian Constitution (the right to equality before the law). While RoPA debars candidates convicted of serious offences from contesting elections for six years after their release from prison, Section 8(4) of the same Act makes an exception for sitting legislators. This grants an unfair advantage by allowing convicted legislators to contest elections, while denying the right to those who are convicted but do not hold office.

Under the present system, political patronage and a 'culture of adjournment' collude to prevent speedy trials of elected representatives. Public prosecution is often ineffective and coloured by vested interests. All in all, the system is wired to push for a favourable outcome for the accused elected representative.

Break the Criminal-Political Nexus

Criminalization of politics does more than just subvert ethics in governance; it hits at the root of public engagement with the system. Not only is this trend highly demoralizing for the general public, it also reduces people's trust in the system and forces them into apathy and disillusionment. Therefore, there is an urgent need to break the criminal-political nexus. This will go a long way towards restoring our people's confidence in the judiciary and in redeeming the commitment of the political class towards justice.

In 2013, I submitted three private members' bills in the Lok Sabha. These aimed to attack the roots of the problem. My first bill proposed to amend RoPA to remove the exception that allows MPs and MLAs/members of legislative council (MLCs) to continue in the legislature even after conviction. The second would set up fast track courts for speedy trial (within ninety days) of criminal cases against all elected representatives. It would bring all MPs, MLAs/ MLCs and members of panchayats and municipalities established under the state Panchayati Raj legislation under the bill's ambit. The third would amend the Code of Criminal Procedure (CCP) to enable independent and effective prosecution.

In a country that is infamous for its snail-paced judiciary and the gargantuan pendency of cases in the subordinate and higher courts, this simple tweak that fast-tracks criminal cases against elected representatives, with a mandate that all relevant cases be adjudicated within ninety days, will go a long way towards resolving the problem. Unlike some other proposals that bar candidates from contesting elections if charged with criminal cases, this solution will not vitiate the presumption of innocence and should be seen as a 'privilege' given to elected representatives—an opportunity to quickly clear their names of malicious or frivolous allegations.

To ensure that these fast track courts do not suffer from the same impediments as regular courts, my bill provides that the number of judges to be appointed to each court must be decided on the basis of an objective criterion that takes into account caseload, pendency and, most importantly, the percentage of cases that remain unresolved after the stipulated deadline of ninety days. This provision will act as a check on the power of the executive to undermine the object of the bill by changing the judicial strength of these courts.

Furthermore, to ensure that the proceedings don't suffer owing to ineffective or biased prosecution, my third bill proposed to increase accountability and transparency in the appointment of prosecutors so as to shield them from political interference. Though the CCP, as it exists, calls for 'consultation' with the judiciary for all appointments to the post of public prosecutor, the requirement has been diluted through amendments in many states. Special public prosecutors are often appointed at the whims and fancies of the government and without adequate reasoning. This is done to suit special interests.

While commenting on the independence of public prosecutors in India, the Law Commission held, in its 197th report, that any legislation that permits the arbitrary appointment of public prosecutors, without proper checks, would violate Article 14 of the Constitution. Therefore, to ensure free and fair trials in courts, it is vital that the existing provisions of the CCP be amended.

My bill mandates the establishment of a separate Directorate of Prosecution in each state, with administrative control over all prosecutors in the state and that is answerable to the home department. It prescribes 'concurrence' with the judiciary for the appointment of prosecutors at all levels. It also sets down an objective criterion to gauge the requirement of prosecutors. The bill will also require a detailed and written explanation from the government about the reasons for each appointment to ensure transparency in the appointment of special public prosecutors.

I believe that even though reforming the entire judicial and political system may require significant investment and political will in the long term, lasting changes can be effected if we attack the roots of the problem in the short term. The private members' bills that I submitted are a step in that direction. Although I recognize that these bills haven't been passed by our Parliament in decades, they do serve as a useful tool to pressure the government.

The perverse trend of criminalization of politics and the inability of the criminal justice system to conduct timely and effective prosecution of offenders are the initiating causes in the causal chain of unfavourable outcomes. Therefore, any attack on the problems that plague our political system must begin with such legislation. The hope is that if enough public support can be drummed up, the government would be compelled to pass legislation to that effect.

This article was first published in *Business Standard* on 26 February 2013

2

DRIVING OUT BLACK MONEY, STEP BY STEP

All that's required now, to reform public funding, is a leader who can pick up the gauntlet and bring about change

The withdrawal of the old ₹500 and ₹1,000 currency notes has been the single-most disruptive economic move since the reforms of 1991. It has been extremely controversial, but not because of popular outrage. In fact, the public reaction to it has been overwhelmingly the opposite, something that much of the mainstream media acknowledged rather belatedly, not to mention grudgingly. The basic problem with our rules on political funding, as in other such areas, is that they evolved in a post-Independence era overflowing with idealism—a good thing, of course, but without the necessary tempering of pragmatism, which is crucial. The end result is that the idealism has remained on the surface (still touted superficially), while the reality has transformed into barely disguised cynicism and hypocrisy.

Opponents of this remonetization have directed their ire at many aspects of it, with arguments that range from valid questions to hysterical denouncements. A reasonable and important aspect of the debate is what effect it will have on illicit 'black' money, especially considering that the nation's politics runs largely on such funds.

Even supporters of remonetization will agree that it could, at most, facilitate the one-time gushing out of unaccounted money. In fact, considering the larger-than-expected amount in old notes that has reportedly been deposited in banks, the extent of this initial success will itself depend on follow-up action by tax and investigative authorities, to catch and freeze illicit deposits.

Sure, the regeneration of black money will be harder now in comparison to earlier instances of remonetization. The increasing requirement of Permanent Account Number (PAN) and Aadhaar cards, the growth of the digital and cashless economy, and the electronic traceability that all these facilitate will create more hurdles for black money than earlier. However, checking large-scale regeneration of black money will need more fundamental reform.

Cleaning Up Political Funding

Nowhere is reform more desperately needed than in the manner in which our politics is funded. Under-the-table political funding is facilitated by vast sums of black money generated from sectors like real estate, mining and primary education, to name a few. There are quid pro quos involved, of course, leading to a vicious cycle of patronage and tolerance of illegality. Cleaning up political funding would have positive ramifications far beyond politics itself.

The idealism in this case was—and is—contempt for the role of money in politics. Tempering it with pragmatism would have recognized the necessity of money to run campaigns, but shifted the emphasis to the legitimacy of political funds and the creation of a level playing field for the role of money. Without that infusion of pragmatism, the rules have focused on expenditure caps in election campaigns that, for decades, remained too artificially low to be realistic.

Even today, though the caps have seen regular and significant increases, the bitter competitiveness of democratic contests provides enormous incentives to oust them. As a result, all that we have achieved is to push campaign expenditure under the carpet and turn it into the biggest magnet for black money.

Similarly, we can no longer fool ourselves by pretending that campaign expenditure caps somehow aid less well-off candidates against wealthier opponents. Sadly, we have achieved the worst of all situations, where virtually all candidates use black money, with wealthier ones obviously getting undue advantages by having more of it. The underlying systemic incentives and controls need rebooting.

Lessons from other democracies should also be instructive. Take the US, for instance. In 2008, the relatively unknown minority candidate, Barack Obama, outspent far wealthier, better-organized and long-established opponents. He was not wealthy himself, but was able to do this because he raised a huge war chest via small donations from the millions of supporters whom he enthused.

It is also clear that while money is a necessary ingredient for modern campaigns, it is far from sufficient by itself. Though Donald Trump is the first billionaire to have ever won the US presidency, ironically it was not his money that gave him the edge. In fact, his campaign is reckoned to have cost half that of Hillary Clinton's! It was not the money that worked for Trump but the strategic positioning of himself at the crest of a wave of resentment and anger. Think what you will of that strategy, but don't blame money for the outcome.

There have been efforts earlier to bring about campaign finance reform in India, but none has come close to getting widespread support. Moreover, most of them suffered from the same bias—of contempt for the use of money in politics, rather than accepting it as a necessity, and regulating its legitimacy and levelling the playing field—that has led to this crisis in the first place.

Campaign Finance Reform

A classic example of campaign finance reform was the Indrajit Gupta Committee of 1998. It had made some pragmatic recommendations, such as the gradual introduction of the state funding of campaigns, limited to parties recognized by the EC as national or state parties. But it had a bizarre aversion to money, insisting that state funding should be in kind, such as rent-free accommodation, fuel for candidates, loudspeakers, and so on, in impractical, excruciating detail.

Though the idea of state funding has occasionally been bandied about in India, it has usually lacked conceptual clarity and, even more importantly, a lack of consensus on the idea itself. Take, for instance, the recommendations by the Law Commission of India in 2015, which came about after lengthy deliberations. Though it contains many useful ideas, they are mostly about incremental improvements in expenditure control during elections. Neither does it recommend state funding, nor does it deal with the roots of black money in campaigns.

The EC has recently taken a stab at the latter, by floating the idea that the ceiling for anonymous political donations be lowered from the present ₹20,000 per donation to ₹2,000. This is one of the most critically needed reforms, since vast sums of black money are funnelled into politics by claiming alleged—and anonymous— donations of ₹19,999 each.

It is legitimate for political parties to want some funds to be collected in cash, even anonymously, for instance, at large rallies where the hustle and bustle make it impractical to do paperwork or collect details. However, that must not be an excuse to claim unrealistic sums. Reducing the ceiling drastically (I would go even further and lower it to ₹500) and limiting this option for only donations received at public rallies, would sharply limit what could be thus collected.

Some sceptics have doubted that this would have much effect. However, it will, since parties would have to demonstrate humongously bigger rallies than at present, of millions of attendees instead of lakhs, to justify the funds being collected; that simply won't happen. Moreover, even if any party were to attempt it, at a ₹500 limit per anonymous donation, the cost of organizing such rallies would exceed the anonymous donations that could be claimed!

More would need to be done to enforce the legitimacy and traceability of funds that find their way into politics. For instance, political parties enjoy tax exemption on the funds they raise. That ought to be limited to only the funds raised from sources that are traceable, legitimately earned and tax-compliant. The enormity of the impact that these would have on cleaning up our politics simply cannot be overstated.

However, the implementation and enforcement of such a fundamental change will need the powers of the EC to be enhanced. Ironically, though political parties are required to have their accounts audited, many simply don't bother with auditing. Moreover, those who do, can get away with brazenly fictitious bookkeeping, audited by friendly accountants, secure in the knowledge that the EC does not actually have the powers to either enforce proper audits or penalize violations. It is shocking that the EC, arguably our most credible constitutional authority, does not have these powers.

There have been proposals to include political parties' accounts under the RTI, in the hope that public shaming and pressure could get them to reform. But a far more effective way would be to empower the EC instead. It would avoid overlapping powers between authorities, and provide for enforcement and remedial measures, rather than mudslinging or prolonged litigation. The EC must be empowered to both enforce audits of political party funds and impose penalties.

These proposed measures all reinforce the intrinsic acceptance that the use of money in election campaigns is natural, but at the same time, also rigidly ensure the legitimacy, traceability and tax-compliant nature of such funds. They would go a long way towards checking black money in politics, not to mention the cascading effects it has in many other sectors.

Level Playing Field

Nevertheless, further reforms would be needed to ensure a level playing field between rich and poor parties and candidates. This is where state funding comes in—an idea which has been deployed in other democracies. In India, it has its share of proponents, but has usually been floated without details of how it would function. The principle of state funding itself needs justification, because some sceptics have questioned why taxpayer funds should be 'wasted' on politics. The answer must lie in the core belief that democracy is a good thing, and that for it to function effectively, the funds used in politics must both be legitimate as well as regulated in a manner that is equitable to rich and poor candidates alike.

Thus far, the regulations to make electoral contests equitable with regard to funding, have relied on campaign expenditure caps that have failed miserably. State funding is the answer to ensuring that equity. Furthermore, the essential element of this equity must focus on levelling the playing field between wealth and popularity.

In other words, state funding must provide a financial boost to parties and candidates that may be popular but are disadvantaged by opponents who are wealthy. The way to do this is to provide state funding as matching grants to the legitimate, traceable and tax-compliant funds raised by parties and candidates. Furthermore, the matching grants must disproportionately reward small donors over big ones. Thus, for instance, for every Aadhaar-corroborated individual donation received between ₹500 and ₹10,000, the state funding could be a matching grant of, say, five times that amount.

This would vastly boost the prospects of parties and candidates that are able to mobilize legitimate, tax-compliant donations from a large number of small donors—which demonstrates their popularity—against opponents that are wealthier or can mobilize large donations from, say, corporates.

Taken together, these measures would radically restructure the nature of political funding in India, change the underlying systemic incentives and put in place effective control systems.

But can all this actually happen?

The rot has gone so deep that thinking Indians find it hard to conceive how politics can function without black money. Thus, even the most well-intentioned of opinion-makers say something along the lines of 'well, of course it would be a good thing to cleanse politics of black money, but it is impossible to achieve in practice; it will never happen.'

It is a good thing, then, that the vast majority of Indians who support remonetization have rather more cut and dried views on black money. In other words, there are huge, hidden reserves of unambiguous support among the public for a radical restructuring of political funding. They are just waiting for a leader who is brazen enough to pick up the gauntlet.

The PM has not only come out in support of the EC's idea to lower the cap for anonymous donations, but reportedly also exhorted his colleagues to support greater transparency in party funding. If his stunning gambit on remonetization is to lead to a lasting legacy of transforming India, he must go boldly where no Indian politician has gone before, and reform political funding.

This article was first published in *Swarajya* on 1 February 2017

3

AUTUMN OF THE PATRIARCH

Dynasty has its uses in politics,
but is being supplanted by modern media

The internal civil war in the Samajwadi Party (SP) got enormous media coverage, along with an analysis of its potential to impact the 2017 Uttar Pradesh elections. Separately, it should also interest us for the possible implications on the future of dynastic political parties in India.

This is only the second time that a dynastic successor in modern Indian politics has seized control from the patriarch. The only other time was in 1995, when a young N.C. Naidu took over the Telugu Desam Party and the chief ministership of undivided Andhra Pradesh from N.T. Rama Rao.

Modern Indian political dynasties got off to a fledgling start in 1929, when Jawaharlal Nehru succeeded his father, Motilal, as president of the Congress party, and got another boost when Indira Gandhi secured that post in 1959, while Nehru was still the PM. But it was not even when Indira Gandhi herself became PM in 1966 that the dynasty took hold—in fact, that was not to happen until the mid '70s.

Since then, of course, India has seen a proliferation of political dynasties. This can be seen through two contrasting perspectives. On the one hand, it is a turning back of the clock, with feudalistic principles now guiding many ostensibly democratic political parties. On the other hand, it can counterintuitively be viewed as a work-in-progress, since two dozen dynasties having influence over the country is arithmetically more democratic than just one.

There has been plenty of analysis on why dynasties work in this most competitive of professions. In summary, two reasons stand out:

the brand value of a dynasty and its grip over party machineries. Journalist and author Mark Tully has written: 'dynasticism appeals to notions of inherited charisma.' Similarly, business and non-profit writer, Ranjani Iyer Mohanty, describes dynastic candidates as giving voters the comfort of 'knowing what to expect, offering a sense of continuity and stability.'

This is instantly understandable to anyone involved in the field of marketing and familiar with the compelling power of brands. Yet, it may be the lesser of the two reasons, with the grip over parties counting for even more. Though there had been a time when the power of a dynasty's brand was far stronger than that of the party, it may no longer hold true. For instance, Indira Gandhi had split the Congress not once but twice, and yet, despite new party symbols, managed to prevail.

However, that era may have passed. According to the New York University's professor of politics, Kanchan Chandra, 'Parties are important. No dynast in these three Parliaments (2004, 2009 and 2014) who has fought outside of a party structure has won.' This, irrespective of the relative brand strengths of SP's founder vis-à-vis his son, explains the bitter tussle for control of the party symbol, which the EC has now awarded to the latter.

Control over parties is also important because of the powerful networks they have built over years. These party networks, nurtured with patronage as well as personal relationships, have traditionally played a vital role in campaigns.

They organize political rallies and put up posters. They also mobilize voters during elections, arranging everything from feasts to enthuse them, to transportation for getting them to voting booths. One reason why nepotism works in politics is that dynasts have long, intergenerational bonds with these party networks.

Beyond Party Networks

Nevertheless, there is increasing evidence that successful modern campaigns must go beyond reliance on such party networks. In

Western democracies, the trend has been visible for more than three decades, with the UK's Margaret Thatcher and the US's Ronald Reagan having famously gone over the heads of their party networks to connect directly with voters.

More recently, technology has provided new tools to relative outsiders to seize control of political parties in innovative ways. Barack Obama in 2008, and Donald Trump last year, exemplified this trend, relying much more on social media (SM) than on their party networks to both take control of their parties and to galvanize voters.

India, too, has begun seeing similar examples. Narendra Modi and Arvind Kejriwal stand out for their leveraging of technology and SM to both transform and transcend their parties. It is no surprise that they, and other SM pioneers like Shashi Tharoor, are mostly first-generation politicians.

It should also not be surprising that dynastic politicians have been among the least enthusiastic users of SM in India. Even younger, tech-savvy scions of political families have been laggards on this front, taking to SM only lately, when its impact could no longer be ignored.

With the inherent advantage of having traditional networks, dynasts have not felt compelled to find new ways to take control of parties or connect with voters. Newcomers with the proverbial fire in their bellies, by contrast, thrive on disruptive alternatives. Using technology to build party support, engage voters and even arrange 'flash mobs' via SM, is entirely natural to this cohort.

None of this signals the impending end of political dynasties in India. The strength of dynastic brands and the control of traditional party networks will continue to matter. But equally, it is becoming increasingly feasible to scale up alternative new brands and networks, and far more rapidly than before. The implications could be momentous.

This article was first published in *The Times of India* on 18 January 2017

4

YOUNG, NOT SO RESTLESS

*Statistics show that younger members of parliament participate
significantly less in the Parliament*

Over the past decade, the arrival, in the Parliament, of a
number of young MPs—fresh-faced, well educated, smart at
parrying TV sound bites, and savvy about the world at large—raised
hopes for a transformation of Indian politics. The hype generated
was always overstated, but has gradually given way to muted
disappointment. Now, pointed questions are beginning to be asked.

Statistics show that younger MPs participate significantly less in
the Parliament, albeit in an atmosphere where the Parliament itself is
mostly gridlocked. Even using a cut-off age of fifty, it turns out that
those who are older participate in debates 40 per cent more often.
The argument, that party hierarchies stifle younger MPs, has some
merit, but is contradicted by the poor performance of even someone
like Rahul Gandhi, who participated in only one discussion in the
15th Lok Sabha, and asked not a single question.

Even setting aside parliamentary participation, why is it that so
few in this cohort are making a name for themselves by proposing
new ideas, or even standing up for something (other than toeing their
party's line)? The answer lies in the sharply increased hierarchical
nature of all political parties, and the propelling of status quoists,
both young and old, into positions of authority, by this structure.

Though India has seen intra-party democracy gradually crumble
since the days of Indira Gandhi, the trend of consolidating power at
the top of the hierarchy has continued unabated in all parties. Since
most parties don't have internal elections for organizational posts
or nominations to contest elections, toeing the hierarchy's line has

become essential to the majority of politicians' survival, let alone success. Once elected to the Parliament, even would-be mavericks are straitjacketed by the ubiquitous party whip. Generally issued for just about any major debate or vote in the Parliament, defiance of the whip is grounds for disqualification as an MP.

India's Top-down Diktat Machine

Many such rules and regulations that make it impractical for politicians to speak their mind were instituted as cures for earlier ills, but the law of unintended consequences has ensured that they have led to new ones. For instance, the election rules for the Rajya Sabha, which used to be by secret ballot, were amended in the past decade to deal with allegations of votes being sold by MLAs, who are the electors. Now, the ballot is open and parties issue whips to their MLAs to vote for their candidates, defiance of which leads to the MLA getting disqualified from the assembly. What the change in law has achieved, besides removing MLAs' choice of whom to vote for, is to incentivize wealthy Rajya Sabha aspirants to deal directly with, and be beholden to, party leaderships instead.

Thus, the party system in India has evolved into a top-down diktat machine, which MPs and MLAs simply don't dare defy. The only rare exceptions are when they perceive an extremely high level of dissonance with their voters and believe it would be suicidal to not defy their party—for example, on the issue of Telangana. Sadly, no other recent issues, including, for instance, the anti-corruption debate, have inspired much outspokenness. This has led to an increasing number of conformists in the Parliament, with the path to success lying clearly in keeping their opinions to themselves, refraining from taking the lead on big issues and otherwise demonstrating their personal loyalty to their leadership.

Younger MPs are no exception to this, having had to struggle and succeed in exactly the same environment. In fact, many would say that they have an additional burden of conformity, by being largely from political families themselves. Patrick French highlighted this in his 2011 book, *India: A Portrait*—while just over a quarter of all MPs entered politics through family connections, that figure rose to two-third for those under forty, and a startling 100 per cent for the under-thirties! This undoubtedly contributes to an ambience of homogeneity and resistance to change.

Ironically, despite the rules encouraging conformity, and younger MPs being additionally conditioned for the status quo by their backgrounds, there are some signs that it is this group that is experimenting with stretching some boundaries. Examples include cross-party advocacy on issues like malnutrition, and initiatives supporting fellowships for young graduates to strengthen MPs' research and staffing.

Even more importantly, outside the glare of spotlights, there is a personal bonhomie among this generation of politicians that cuts across party lines and is reminiscent of an earlier, less polarized era. At the very least, this fosters a certain private candour that cuts through public adherence to party diktats. Perhaps, this holds the promise of future cooperation, which is so crucially missing in this age of coalition politics.

This article was first published in *Outlook* on 5 August 2013

5

NOW REFORM POLITICAL FUNDING

*If we have the will, here's how to make a
lasting impact on black money*

The two-weeks-old demonetization tsunami is still reverberating through the nation's socio-economic fabric. It will be months before its impact can be fully understood, but the economic and political landscape has already been rearranged. Political bickering over long bank and ATM queues dominated media reports for the first two weeks. Now, there is increasing coverage on the expected benefits—or lack thereof, depending on which side you are on—as well as various short- and long-term effects on the economy. This chapter will focus on how to cleanse politics of illicit, tax-evaded 'black money'.

It is bizarre that some otherwise reasonable people have said that demonetization will not impact black money. Sure, the currency portion of illicit assets is relatively small, with much more held in gold, real estate, etc. But being, by far, the most fungible, cash is the most crucial part of the black economy. And it is by no means insignificant, with an estimated ₹3 lakh crore and perhaps more now expected to be extinguished. This one-time flushing of a chunk of black money is a significant blow to its users, but a lasting impact requires several other steps. It would be good for the government to tackle, head-on, such whispered allegations that agents are arranging to rehabilitate some of this cash, supposedly through Jan Dhan accounts and suchlike. Quick disproval, or punitive action if true, would add to the credibility of demonetization.

The good news is that unlike 1978, when the last demonetization saw black money get hit but come back roaring, the ground realities are very different now. Mandatory linkage to PAN and Aadhaar cards for most transactions will be one of the fundamental ways to check the regeneration of black money. But the single biggest step would be to start cleaning up political funding. Some years ago, the Law Commission of India had sought public suggestions on electoral reforms, whereupon I had given written recommendations to it and to the EC. Though the Law Commission's subsequent 2015 report contained many laudable ideas for electoral transparency, its chapter on 'election finance reform' stopped short of anything truly radical or transformative.

The most important aspect of election finance reform is to shift the focus from limiting campaign expenses to rigidly enforcing the legitimacy and traceability of the money trail. Our decades-long, utopian thrust on capping campaign expenses has not worked, and has merely pushed money under the carpet. This is the root cause, the motivation for black money, and for the mechanisms that generate it. The fear that allowing higher campaign expenses would somehow undermine democracy is unfounded, and there are better ways of ensuring a level playing field than expense caps. In any event, for all practical purposes, the caps are meaningless and have only incentivized the use of unsavoury funds from dubious sources.

The reality is that money is necessary, but far from sufficient, ingredient for electoral success. Ironically, even billionaire Donald Trump's successful campaign relied on a budget that was half of his opponent's! Rather than expense caps, it is far more important to ensure that campaign funds are from traceable, tax-compliant sources. Thus, the floor of ₹20,000, below which political contributions can be received anonymously, must be drastically lowered. This is the single greatest window of abuse, with huge sums of black money being transacted without any traceability. Though I had earlier favoured a floor of ₹5,000, I now believe it needs to be ₹1,000 or even ₹500. That would allow genuine on-the-spot donations, say, at political rallies, but make it far harder to channel large amounts of illicit funds via countless 'nameless donors'.

Next, there must be state funding to help level the playing field between the wealthy and the popular. Like elsewhere, our state funding should be given as matching funds to candidates and parties, equivalent to the amount of traceable, tax-compliant funds that they raise. In fact, small donations must be further incentivized over big ones, say, with five-times matching funds for every individual ₹1,000 of tax-compliant funds raised. Together, all this will be a boon to non-wealthy but popular candidates and parties.

Finally, audits of candidates' and parties' accounts must be made mandatory, and the tax exemptions they now receive be limited to funds that are traceable and tax-compliant. Most importantly, the EC's powers must be enhanced to enforce such audits, along with punitive powers ranging from mild penalties to disqualifications. It is amazing that the EC does not have these powers.

The past three months have been momentous, with the passage of the previously intractable GST bill, surgical strikes across the Line of Control (LoC), and now demonetization. Like its policies or not, it is undeniable that after a period of drift, the Modi government seems to be on a roll.

This new, 'no longer business as usual' scenario is aptly described by an aphorism from *The Wizard of Oz*, 'We're not in Kansas anymore.' So, how out-of-the-box is the PM prepared to be? As it happens, he reportedly mooted the idea of the state funding of elections at last week's all-party meeting. Irrespective of our political leanings, this deserves support and championing by thinking citizens.

This article was first published in *The Times of India* on 23 November 2016

6

HOW THE BHARATIYA JANATA PARTY SECURED POLE POSITION

To remain the central pillar of Indian politics,
it must ensure opponents don't gang up

With the electoral results of early 2017 across five states, the Bharatiya Janata Party (BJP) and PM Modi have once again secured pole position in Indian politics. This had happened earlier too, under Vajpayee and after Modi's massive win in 2014, but national- or state-level setbacks followed. Is the shift more structural this time around? And what does the future hold for the Congress and regional parties?

Most of PM Vajpayee's 1999–2004 tenure had felt like an increasingly post-Congress era. This was right in the middle of a twenty-five-year period of coalition governments, but even on the eve of the 2004 general elections, very few considered a Congress revival likely.

Nevertheless, the Congress did revive and ran India for ten more years. Can it do so again? To put it mildly, the Congress leadership today does not give the impression of being up to that task. Even the big win in Punjab is being credited to its regional satrap, not its national leaders. It has been decimated in the heartland and, with reduced vote shares and just short of majorities, outmanoeuvred in forming governments in Goa and Manipur.

The Congress today suffers from apolitical, out-of-touch and wrong instincts at its highest levels. Take, for instance, its visceral opposition to demonetization, which was immensely popular at the grass roots (even if not enough to fully overcome anti-incumbency in two states). The lack of meritocracy, evidenced by many bright younger Congressmen and women who have been held back for years, has taken a huge toll on its capabilities.

This is the gap that the Aam Aadmi Party (AAP) was widely expected to fill, but did not. In Goa, its reported growth turned out to be a damp squib, and in Punjab, much less than the hype. So, at least for now, AAP will not be the new Congress.

As for the BJP, despite being hit hard by anti-incumbency in Goa and Punjab, its success in Uttar Pradesh was resounding, with a whopping 40 per cent vote share. What distinguished its campaign was a resolute return to 2014's development mantra. That focus had somewhat wavered in the interim, such as during the 2015 Bihar elections when the Dadri incident dominated the discourse, but is now clearly back on centre stage.

That is not to say that other local issues or caste equations did not matter in Uttar Pradesh. They did, and the BJP was adept at countering others' alliances and cross-caste tie-ups with a canny ground game of its own. But the overarching theme that secured the landslide was its 'big tent' and aspirational development message. That seems to have helped it grow structurally, beyond its traditional base, attracting younger voters across the board.

It is not as if others did not try the same strategy—for instance, SP's 'Kaam Bolta Hai' slogan. But hoping to succeed by co-opting others' strategies, despite the baggage of years of entrenched casteist politics and governance, was a case of cognitive dissonance.

Strange Bedfellows

Even long-term sceptics of the BJP are beginning to admit that the PM succeeded in marketing his all-aboard strategy in Uttar Pradesh. One of the best-known faces among Indian liberal journalists told me that the party's victory in heavily Muslim-dominated constituencies indicates an unprecedented breakthrough for it.

What all this means is that in more and more places in India, it will take an alliance of all other significant players to stop the BJP, as happened in Bihar. In fact, Bihar's astute CM Nitish Kumar has already said so, giving credit for the Uttar Pradesh results to both 'people's satisfaction with demonetization' and the lack of a Bihar-like mahagathbandhan coalition.

How likely are such all-except-BJP coalitions in various parts of the country? Desperation is the mother of invention, and calls have already been sounded for a Uttar Pradesh coalition in 2019 of not just SP and the Congress, but also the Bahujan Samaj Party and others. However, though politics does make strange bedfellows, the likelihood of some of these combinations stretches credulity. For instance, the coming together of the main Dravidian parties, or of Bengal's leftist parties with the Trinamool Congress on the same platform, defy common sense.

When it comes to parties like the Biju Janata Dal (BJD), the core base is the non-Congress voter that the late Biju Patnaik nurtured over decades, through various party iterations. The BJD was founded in 1997–98 as a BJP ally, but has been unaligned since 2009. Meanwhile the BJP, after years of languishing as a distant third in Odisha, has recently surged to a credible second place in the state-wide local elections.

Other offshoots of the erstwhile Janata Dal have associated with the Congress, like in Bihar. But in early 2017, BJD President Naveen Patnaik initiated disciplinary proceedings against a senior MP for suggesting that a coalition with the Congress could be considered.

At any rate, if the BJP has indeed become entrenched as the central pillar of Indian politics, then its stratagem should be obvious. Where it already leads in vote share, all it needs to do is manoeuvre in a way that all its opponents don't gang up. In these elections, besides the thrust on broad-basing its appeal, there was already some evidence of just such a game plan.

This article was first published in *The Times of India* on 16 March 2017

THREE

ECONOMY:
IN THE ERA OF MODINOMICS

The current debates between contrasting economic philosophies repeatedly find resonance in history. For instance, the differing economic approaches advocated by Julius Caesar and Cato the Younger, 2,000 years ago, have an eerie similarity to some of the arguments between the left and the right today.

To my mind, there are two crucial lessons from these debates that have taken place over the millennia, for those who would govern, lead or advocate economic ideas—one, that any economy's fundamental soundness will depend on regularly having to swallow bitter pills that will be unpopular, at least in the short term; and two, that only administering bitter pills, sound though they may be for the long run, without making some concessions to populism, will risk ejecting one from having any say in the matter.

For more than a quarter of a century now, India's economy has been opening up. This has not happened at a uniform pace, and, in fact, has sputtered and lurched all through this period. There has been, however, a broad consensus, across the political spectrum, regarding the need for such reforms. Nevertheless, adherence by political parties to that consensus has been fickle, depending on whether they have been in government or in opposition.

Even when in government, political parties have not always been able push along the reform agenda smoothly, due to resistance from their own backbenches as well as from coalition allies. To a large extent, the economic reforms that did happen, were either precipitated by crisis or were conducted with some stealth by the top echelons of the governments of the day.

The Modi era has seen a transition to a more overt championing of reforms from the head of the government. This was a natural corollary to his terms as a state CM who was arguably seen as the most reformist among his peers. And yet, despite his government's epoch-making majority in the Lok Sabha, it has not been as smooth sailing as some had expected. In large part, that is a function of our democratic system, whereby several key initiatives have floundered in the Rajya Sabha, where the government does not have a majority.

In shedding off its partly socialist legacy—where 'profit' was considered a dirty word, private entrepreneurship distrusted, and humongous amounts of wealth destroyed by public sector entities with ambiguous objectives—India's economy has once again emerged as one that counts globally. Though still far from the clout it enjoyed before the colonial era, India is, nonetheless, already being counted as one of the major economic engines of the world.

Ironically, the domestic view of the nation's economy is noticeably more pessimistic than how the rest of the world views it. Despite the return of relatively high growth rates, as well as stunning improvements on indices like the World Bank's Ease of Doing Business (EoDB) index, many at home continue to carp about it.

This may partly be due to very high expectations having been set, by which standard, even rather dramatic reforms may seem inadequate. It is also undoubtedly influenced by several major crises, such as in job creation and bank defaults, which have taken years to get this serious. The challenge for those who would revitalize India's economy remains in achieving that balancing act between urgent populist pressures and important, but painful, long-term reforms.

1

INDIA'S MARKET PHOBIA

Instead of seeking to block the operation of markets,
we must harness them

In 2016, when the Karnataka and Delhi state governments 'banned' surge pricing by taxi aggregators like Ola and Uber, they were entirely in sync with India's long-cherished tradition of populist measures against market forces. That it didn't solve the problem of inadequate public transport—in fact, compounding it by inhibiting the supply of more taxis at peak hours, albeit at higher prices—was almost beside the point.

Ironically, at other times, such instincts have worked in the opposite direction, such as in 2014, when the Ministry of Civil Aviation attempted to stipulate a minimum airfare for every route in order to 'ensure that no airline in future goes into losses'. That was in the backdrop of efficient new airlines out-competing and undercutting inefficient ones.

It would be foolish to dismiss Indian politicians' knee-jerk anti-market instincts without comprehending the underlying rationale, for they are anything but superficial. Scepticism about trade and commerce goes back, at least, to that epitome of private enterprise, the East India Company, which became a symbol of monopoly, extortionate practices and the capitulation of Indian public interest.

It can even be traced back much further in our ethos, to the fourth century BCE, when Kautilya's statecraft advocated large doses of statist dominance in the economy of the Mauryan empire. In more recent times, cronyism has sullied the reputation of markets.

Cronyism in India is not just limited to national mega-scams, but is part of the everyday experience of the average citizen. Even in remote villages, every Indian is familiar with the favoured contractor or tout grabbing the lion's share of the benefits of ostensibly market transactions, to the public's detriment. It is these distortions that are erroneously but widely perceived as free markets.

Populism was always inevitable in the world's largest, most diverse democracy. What also contributed to this was the instant universal adult franchise that we acquired with our Constitution. Most other democracies had got there after decades, sometimes centuries—from originally allowing only land-owning males to vote, to gradually enfranchising more and more sections of the citizenry.

By contrast, India went from populism counting for very little in the colonial era, to suddenly mattering hugely to political leaders who needed to win over large numbers of voters.

Nevertheless, India is a nation feted for its people's entrepreneurial skills. Our entrepreneurs are counted not just among the global corporate elite, but also the millions of small businesses around the country. They bridge the many gaps between demand and supply, often with innovative 'jugaad' solutions.

Understanding Free Markets

The reality is that no nation in modern times has successfully bucked market forces to achieve affluence for its people. Even the nominally communist China, which, till 1980, had a similar per capita profile as India, now has an economy five times bigger than India's, by embracing markets much more enthusiastically.

That is not to say that free markets are the be all and end all of policymaking. Political philosopher and Harvard University professor Michael Sandel writes compellingly about this in his bestseller *What Money Can't Buy: The Moral Limits of Markets*— he questions the pervasiveness of markets in all areas of life, but does not question the efficacy of markets. His arguments are moral, ranging from the mundane (is it acceptable to have fast track queues for business class passengers?) to reiterating ethical redlines, such as the ban on the sale of human organs.

While developed countries have the luxury of debating the outer limits of markets, developing ones must grapple with the inevitability of needing to harness them for their day-to-day economic needs. Like the legendary King Canute*, India's politicians need to recognize that the market forces of supply and demand can no more be wished away by diktat than the waves pounding our shores.

Arthur Brooks, a leading conservative thinker, bestselling author and president of the American Enterprise Institute, has written, 'Market forces tend to win out even when we don't want them to; good intentions are no guarantee of good results, and we can't change behaviour just by passing a law against something we don't like.'

Therein lies the kernel of what Indian decision makers need to grasp—not to wish that market forces didn't exist or to check them, but to tailor policy to harness them for the common good, and to correct for market failures and rectify inequity.

Markets allocate scarce resources efficiently, if not equitably, by reconciling supply and demand through the price mechanism. Tampering with prices destroys that efficiency. The way to rectify inequities is not by interfering in markets and blocking prices, but by targeted subsidies for the underprivileged.

Thus, for instance, rent assistance for the poor is a much better idea than rent control, but that requires funds to be allocated, whereas some politicians still believe they can get away by promising a free lunch. However, besides taxation, funds can also be availed by cross-subsidizing—for example, levying a fee on airlines flying lucrative sectors and offering that as a subsidy to fly uneconomical routes.

Tinkering with prices is an easy source of magnanimity for politicians, but it mostly only succeeds in driving transactions

*Canute was a Danish ruler of the eleventh century. The story of King Canute and the tide, written in the twelfth century by an English historian, depicts how the sea waves continued to break on the shore and wet the king's feet and robes, despite his 'command' to them to not do so. It's often cited in the context of not being able to 'stop the tide'.

underground, while having a decidedly deleterious effect on investment and economic growth. It is exactly this kind of market interference that creates conditions for corruption to flourish.

This article was first published in *The Times of India* on 11 May 2016

2

MOODY'S: GLASS HALF FULL

Upgrade vindicates fundamentals, but for the economy to take off, bold reform steps are needed

In November 2017, when Moody's, one of the world's top three credit ratings agencies, raised India's sovereign rating after nearly fourteen years, the responses to it demonstrated the nation's sharply divided politics. While the government understandably tom-tommed it as proof that its policies were succeeding, Opposition leaders almost universally derided it.

In reality, it is indeed a vindication of improvements in the fundamentals of India's economy. It will ease access to credit, help attract investment and boost job creation. While this is surely cause for some celebration, hubris is best avoided. There is still immense struggle ahead for a long way if India is to overcome its economic and human development challenges.

Ratings agencies are far from infallible. Indeed, Moody's itself had been criticized for not catching the problems at Lehman Brothers, the Wall Street firm it had rated highly and whose collapse in 2008 precipitated the global financial crisis. However, they were not alone, with the other two ratings majors—Fitch, and Standard & Poor's (S&P)—also being in the same boat.

Subsequently, they have had to work hard to re-establish credibility. For instance, S&P claimed to 'have spent approximately $400 million to reinforce the integrity, independence and performance of our ratings. We also brought in new leadership, instituted new governance and enhanced risk management.'

Regulatory changes, too, have tightened norms and increased oversight, such as the US Dodd-Frank Wall Street Reform and

Consumer Protection Act. Though some critics still pan the ratings process, the fact is that risk evaluations by independent agencies remain crucial to how capital is allocated throughout the world. Finally, the proof of the pudding is in the eating: no respectable lender or investor of consequence will act without a credit rating.

Thus, questioning ratings firms' evaluations might have been justifiable a few years ago, or even today in relevant industry or academic forums with specific procedural challenges, but sneering at them broadly, that too only when triggered by the country's rating upgrade, reeks of partisanship. In fact, since some of the critics would gladly have turned metaphorical cartwheels to get a ratings uptick if they were in government, it might even be seen as churlish.

Historic Fork in the Road

The ratings improvement ought not to have come as a surprise to any neutral observer of the Indian economy. On several occasions, this author for one, has bucked the generally gloomy trend of commentary since demonetization, to recognize contrarian, positive changes taking place. There were also unmissable external clues, including praise from the IMF and India's unprecedented thirty-place jump in the World Bank's annual Ease of Doing Business (EoDB) Index in 2017.

Moody's report has forecast a GDP growth rate turnaround from last quarter's 5.7 per cent (a three year low) to 6.7 per cent for FY 2018, 7.5 per cent for FY 2019, and 'similarly robust' levels from 2019 onwards. If this turns out to be the case, it will bode well for the nation.

However, India's potential for growth is even higher, as is our desperate need for it. China, the only other billion-plus population nation, had a similar per capita income level as India in the late '70s. But four decades of sustained high growth has made the size of its economy five times of India's. This has helped China to do much better than us in reducing poverty and creating jobs.

India has missed the bus on earlier occasions to put policies in place for sustained high growth rates, but now, there is a historic fork in the road. Chinese growth has been plateauing, and global financial markets currently deem its commitment to reform inadequate. China's aggressive foreign policy has also raised hackles. Both economics and geopolitics have conspired to give us another opportunity to get our act together.

For that to happen, many significant hurdles will have to be overcome. Take, for example, the PM's declared goal of getting India into the top fifty of the EoDB Index. Despite dramatic improvements this year on several measures, India still ranks a lowly #181 (out of 190 nations) on dealing with construction permits, and #164 on enforcement of contracts.

Some of these could be tackled administratively and steps are apparently already being taken to have dedicated courts for commercial disputes. Others, like the GST, will require even more simplification than the many steps already taken in recent weeks. If 90 per cent items could be taxed at one rate, say 15 per cent, and filings and refunds further simplified, the effects would be substantial.

However, the really big-ticket items will require legislative changes, and therein lies the rub. Two of the biggest hurdles to investment, economic growth and job creation are the impossibly complicated land acquisition law, and the obsolete, counterproductive labour laws.

For now, this government seems to have concluded, like its predecessors, that it would cost too much political capital to take these head on. So, it has been left to the states, a few of which are attempting tentative, baby steps.

Demonstrable success in any state would stir competition and emulation by others, gradually boosting the national economy. But for a dramatic and quicker raising of the trajectory, there is no alternative to taking the bull by the horns in the Parliament.

This article was first published in *The Times of India* on 21 November 2017

3

THESE ARE TEETHING TROUBLES

Demonetization and the Goods & Services Tax will boost economy in the long run; job growth is less assured

There's much discussion about the state of the economy these days. This is natural, considering the resurgent GDP growth rates of the past couple of years, which had earned India the tag of the fastest-growing large economy, have come down in the past three quarters. On top of that is a continuing dearth of private sector investment and job creation.

The debate is more often black-and-white rather than nuanced, but the issues are important and deserve to be understood better. Much of the criticism seems centred on the effects of demonetization, its apparent failure to curb black money and the teething troubles of the GST. While there are elements of truth in those views, the reality is somewhat more complex.

The manner in which demonetization was projected to extinguish black money played out rather differently. It had been argued that up to ₹3 lakh crore of illicit, tax-evaded money would not come back into the banking system. Many had found this argument credible (this writer among them). But that was not to be, with the Reserve Bank of India (RBI) reporting that only ₹16,000 crore out of the ₹15.44 lakh crore of discontinued currency was not deposited in banks.

There were also rumours that most tax evaders gamed the system and found loopholes, especially via large numbers of unused bank accounts of the poor, to get their money laundered and back into the system. However, there is more to this than meets the eye.

Recall that in the weeks after demonetization, the RBI kept

changing the rules for depositing and withdrawing cash, 'know your customer' norms and suchlike. Though there was criticism of those frequent changes, what was happening was a cat-and-mouse game between hucksters trying to launder black money and the authorities trying to clamp down on it.

It now bears watching as to how much of that deposited money gets entangled and inaccessible as a result of the stricter norms. Data mining by the taxman, linking PAN cards to Aadhaar and other such measures will undoubtedly cause grief to those who cannot legitimately explain the source of those funds.

In any event, if you think demonetization did not have much impact on curbing black money, all you need to do is speak to real estate developers and private, for-profit college proprietors. Other than political funding, these two sectors were arguably the biggest users of black money in the economy. While they had been facing challenges in recent years, demonetization, and subsequently GST, dealt a severe blow to their cash-based business models.

In fact, all cash-heavy sectors have suffered from the one-two punch of demonetization and GST, with the latter's impact likely to sustain due to its inbuilt systemic pressures for compliance. Those businesses that can survive a transition from being tax-evasive to being tax-compliant, will nevertheless suffer higher costs, lower demand and thinner margins. This has certainly contributed to the economic slowdown. The point is that you cannot have your cake and eat it too, by simultaneously claiming that demonetization and GST have hurt the economy, while also insisting that black money did not get affected.

The Tectonic Shift

The relevant questions now are: how long will the economy take to recover from the disruption of demonetization? How long will the initial glitches of GST implementation last? And, what will it take to boost investment and jobs?

The first is partly answered by the Economic Survey-II of

2016–17. It showed, first, a monthly dip in the Mahatma Gandhi National Rural Employment Guarantee Act (MGNREGA) demand for job work due to the demonetization cash crunch. Thereafter, because other jobs were likely disrupted, there was a significant surge in MGNREGA work, which lasted nearly three months before returning to normal. That probably indicates a settling down of economic forces impacting the poorest citizens, albeit at a lower level of growth than before November.

On GST, some critics harp that it was too big a second disruption to have been launched so soon after the first, but most agree that its impact will be very positive in the long run. The current pain of its clogged online system, declined returns and extended deadlines is testing the government's bandwidth. Nevertheless, according to the World Bank's country head, GST is a 'tectonic shift' that may propel India into an '8 per cent-plus growth rate'.

This will require investment. Public investment has been picking up, with increases on infrastructure, defence, railways, and now rural electrification, beyond the FY 2017 revised estimates. Foreign direct investment (FDI) has also been growing steadily, setting a new record last fiscal.

But domestic private investment remains in a funk. Boosting confidence and competitiveness will require easing credit flows. This is easier said than done, considering the accumulated mess in the banking system, though inflation is still low enough to drop interest rates. Devaluing the rupee could be another option to boost exports.

Growth is likely to bounce back as the effects of GST kick in. Though job creation will increase as well, the stark reality is that because of technology, automation and disintermediation, 8 per cent (or even 10 per cent) GDP growth no longer supports as many jobs as it used to. Radical measures, such as UBI, will need to be considered.

This article was first published in *The Times of India* on 27 September 2017

4

LEAST BAD, MOST TRANSFORMATIVE

The Goods & Services Tax in its present form is not perfect, but nevertheless profoundly good

Too often we disparage the good because it is not perfect. There is no better, or more ironic, demonstration of this than some of the whingeing about the GST.

Of course, by now we should be inured to the spectacle of political parties in the Opposition stridently opposing the very same issues they had championed when in government, as well as the parties in government pushing through the initiatives they had vehemently opposed when in Opposition. But what is remarkable about the GST is the Opposition parties disapproving what they have quite recently not just agreed and given shape to, while being in the Opposition, but also voted for in the Parliament.

That process lasted more than two and a half years on the home stretch, from the December 2014 reintroduction of the GST Bill in the Parliament till just hours before the midnight launch on 1 July 2017, with last-minute revisions to the rates on some items. Overall, the process had taken eighteen years since being conceptualized by PM Vajpayee's economic advisory panel.

The nearly two-decades long journey saw different actors rise to the occasion at different times, laying the groundwork for a fundamental rejig of India's indirect taxation system. For instance, it saw the sagacity of Vajpayee, who assigned the task of designing the GST to a committee headed by Asim Dasgupta, a PhD in economics from the MIT, then serving as the finance minister of communist Bengal.

Also on display were the brave attempts, without requisite

support in the Parliament, by PM Dr Manmohan Singh and his finance ministers, Palaniappan Chidambaram and Pranab Mukherjee. They first mentioned the GST in the 2006 Budget and, in 2011, introduced the bill. As with many important initiatives during the UPA's hapless decade, the GST did not pass. Nonetheless, its listing in the Parliament put a crucial building block in place, making it difficult thereafter for the Congress to oppose its passage beyond a point.

However, it needed PM Narendra Modi's massive electoral successes, not just in the 2014 general election that gave him the numbers in the Lok Sabha, but also in subsequent state elections that, in turn, have been adding to his numbers in the Rajya Sabha, for the GST to become feasible. And even after that, it took his steely-eyed determination to leave a lasting legacy, and Finance Minister Arun Jaitley's considerable strategic and negotiating acumen, to make the GST finally happen.

A Suboptimal Version

None of the above means that the GST in its present form is perfect; in fact, it's far from it. It is not the simple, one-rate, one-set-of-documentation, national tax originally envisaged. The give-and-take process of reaching a final iteration that could get sufficient votes in the Parliament of the planet's largest, most diverse democracy, took a toll. The best description of the GST now is that it is the least bad of all the versions that stood a chance of being legislated.

But why should we be excited about what some call a 'suboptimal version'? The answer lies in welcoming that, which, even if not perfect, is profoundly good. The GST immediately replaces more than a dozen existing taxes. Although not as simple as it should ideally have been (and perhaps can evolve to be in the future), the GST today nevertheless dramatically simplifies India's indirect taxes, as well as the ease of doing business.

Furthermore, it removes the cascading effect of taxes on the vast majority of items consumed by Indians. In doing so, it creates inbuilt incentives for compliance, with evaders willy-nilly having to bear higher input costs than their GST-compliant peers and competitors.

Most importantly, it finally unites India as a single market after seven decades of Independence. The value of that cannot be overstated, with incalculable benefits likely to emerge, as we no longer have to hobble with fragmented regional markets and disparate tax regulations.

In some ways, the implementation of the GST has the potential to be as transformative for India's economy as the Interstate Commerce Act was for the US. That was enacted in 1887, more than a century after the US independence, to overcome regional monopolies by railway companies. Paving the way for federal rather than state regulations in a host of sectors, it unified the US's fragmented domestic markets and helped propel it to become the largest economy in the world.

So, why would an Opposition party, which loses no opportunity to brag about having first moved the GST Bill in the Parliament, forfeit the opportunity to share the credit at its gala launch? The reason is not cussedness, as some believe; it is, instead, cold political calculus.

Whether right or wrong, their calculation is that the complexity of such a radical tax makeover will lead to serious glitches and sustained dissatisfaction—in other words, ideal circumstances to stir the political pot, but only if you have kept adequate distance from the celebrations.

This approach, by the principal Opposition party—which is essentially, waiting for this government to trip up—has been, more or less, its only strategy for the past four years. It has not worked so far, and there is no reason to believe that it now suddenly will. To be relevant again, they must go beyond hoping for their nemesis to implode.

This article was first published in *The Times of India* on 5 July 2017

5

LET THE MAHARAJA GO

The Air India disinvestment will erase doubts about the
National Democratic Alliance government's will to reform

There is a buzz in the air about the possible privatization of Air India—that quintessential public sector white elephant. Since 1991, this has been seen as the ultimate litmus test of every Indian government's reformist convictions, which none has yet managed to conquer.

That is ironic, since, on several occasions, the respective governments of the day have managed far more substantial economic reforms. Consider two examples from either end of the twenty-six years since liberalization. First, PM P.V. Narasimha Rao's dismantling of industrial licencing was much more impactful than the government getting out of any one company or sector.

Similarly, the enactment of the GST by the present government heralds a seismic shift in India's economy. While Rao deftly used India's looming international repayments default to push through his reform, Modi had to manage his economic magnum opus without any such crisis for cover.

The former is often appreciated for his shrewd use of the old adage to never waste a good crisis, and the latter deserves similar kudos for sheer persistence—for, the GST did not arrive on autopilot. No stone was left unturned to make it happen, despite many setbacks along the way, including widespread rumours last year that the government was no longer serious about it.

Nevertheless, to investors and markets, there is something sexy about privatizing a marquee public sector undertaking (PSU) that does not seem to be matched by more structural reform, at least in the short term.

This could be for a variety of reasons—one being that the fiscal benefits of privatizing a prominent PSU boondoggle are immediately visible. The bleeding of public finances, which has been stanched, may be relatively small compared to, say, the fiscal deficit, but it is more or less undisputed, whereas agreeing on the exact long-term benefits of a deeper reform is usually beset with many ifs and buts.

Despite sporadic PSU sell-offs, it has long been known that India finds it difficult to decisively put behind decades of misguided government efforts at running commercial enterprises. Even using the term 'privatization' has proved a taboo, with euphemisms like 'strategic disinvestment' being favoured instead.

Other attempts at political correctness have included reliance on PPPs as an alternative to encouraging outright private sector investment. This camouflage opened the doors for private investment into previously forbidden areas such as infrastructure, where the gap between what is needed and what is available from public coffers is gargantuan. However, the results have been discouraging, mostly due to the public sector partners' bureaucratic DNA overpowering their role as the fig leaf in these projects.

That such subterfuge was felt necessary despite the desperate need for private investment, says a lot about Indian politicians' diffidence about selling reforms on merit and logic. It should be instructive that reformist legends like Thatcher and Reagan were not alone in having to market their policies. Even autocratic China's Deng Xiaoping, who otherwise had no need to persuade the Chinese public about anything much, turned salesman for economic reforms.

Government's Reformist Credentials

There are indications that change is in the air. Modi's aggressive marketing of his Aadhaar-linked rejig of the cooking gas subsidy, as well as his political pitch for the GST during the 2017 state election campaigns, augur well. If enough of his colleagues take the cue (not to mention down-and-out Opposition leaders looking for a new game plan), it might even represent a turning point.

Taking stock of this government's track record on economic reforms, one would have to acknowledge not just the once-in-a-generation GST, but also a bunch of other measures, including mid-level efforts on both the legislative front, such as the one permitting more FDI in the insurance sector, as well as executive fiats, like the recent one abolishing the Foreign Investment Promotion Board altogether.

There are a number of other such measures, such as deregulating diesel pricing, the bankruptcy law, and permitting the private sector to invest in railways and defence, and back into commercial coal mining. But there remain a number of items pending on investors' and markets' wish lists, including labour law reform, deregulation of kerosene and fertilizer pricing, and many more.

When many commentators were critical of the government's cautious approach to reforms back in 2015 and 2016, they may not have fully understood the dynamics of political capital. For instance, its lack of numbers in the Rajya Sabha could not be overcome, leading to an early setback in the ambitious attempt to redo the land acquisition act.

However, irrespective of whether or not commentators have given enough credit to this government's economic reforms in the meantime, they can, today, rightfully ask for greater boldness from it—and the PM, his pockets bulging with the most political capital he has ever had till now, would do well to heed them.

On Air India, Jaitley was reported to have said that if the private sector could run 86 per cent of civil aviation, it could very well run 100 per cent, and without a ₹50,000 crore public subsidy for one airline. If that sentiment is translated into action, it would dramatically change the perception about this government's reformist credentials.

This article was first published in *The Times of India* on 7 June 2017

6

CHECKS AND BALANCES

Permitting tax authorities to conduct raids without the due process will be disastrous

Having elections to decide who is to govern us meets only the most basic definition of a democracy. However, at a deeper level, democracies require checks and balances in governance. Otherwise, no matter how free and fair the elections, they would become autocracies with periodic changes of leadership.

The proposal in the 2017 Budget, to amend Section 132 of the Income Tax (IT) Act is an example of this. The amendment would do away with the requirement for IT officials to demonstrate that they had 'reason to believe' that violations existed, or that the assessee would not comply, before conducting a search and seizure 'raid'.

The danger in this is obvious. Without having to show that they had good reasons for raids, there is nothing to prevent IT officials from conducting them arbitrarily. 'Harassment' and 'rent-seeking'—the terms economists use for corruption—are sure to follow.

Nevertheless, it is worth taking stock of the opposite arguments as well. Checks and balances are meant to prevent the autocratic, mindless or subjective exercise of authority, but not to block its legitimate, justifiable application.

So, where does the Indian government's crackdown on IT evaders stand? The statistics clearly show that the pace has been considerably stepped up in the past two years. For instance, the number of raids in the first half of 2016, at 148, was nearly triple of the fifty-five in the first half of 2015.

Similarly, cash, jewellery and other assets seized during raids in the first seven months of 2016, at ₹330 crore, was more than

300 per cent of the same period in 2015. And unpaid taxes surrendered by assessees in 2016 were ₹3,360 crore, a more-than-50 per cent increase over 2015.

These, however, are paltry figures. Only 37 million of India's 1.3 billion people filed tax returns in 2015–16. They included barely 41 per cent of the 42 million people employed in the formal sector and only a third of the 56 million engaged in the informal sector. This is exacerbated by the large number of tax cases tied up in disputes. In 2016, the tally of disputed cases was nearly 67,000 in the SC and HCs, 1.53 lakh in the IT Appellate Tribunals, and 3.7 lakh with IT commissioners (appeals).

On top of that, in 2017, there was a spike on account of demonetization. The unprecedented number and amount of deposits since 8 November led to speculation about the laundering of black money.

In fact, this represents a unique opportunity for tax authorities, with a vast new database to scrutinize for possible tax evasion. If done swiftly, there is immense potential for not only identifying and confiscating black money, but also bringing large numbers of new assessees into the tax net.

Overcoming Judicial Hurdles

However, it was never going to be easy to rapidly scale up such scrutiny or, indeed, conduct raids. It is not simply a matter of allocating more resources for it, but also having to deal with judicial hurdles. As the Finance Bill explains: 'certain judicial pronouncements have created ambiguity in respect of the disclosure of "reason to believe" or "reason to suspect" recorded by the income tax authority to conduct a search under Section 132.'

But therein lies the rub. If judges have imposed constraints on raids because of unconvincing reasons to believe that they were justified, then it is almost inevitable they will find fault with completely doing away with all justification! However, the executive and legislative branches may decide to abjure cumbersome procedural requirements in the interest of efficiency, which must pass the test of natural justice and constitutional guarantees in order to deter the judicial branch from overturning it.

The answer to dealing with judicial hurdles in stepping up tax enforcement does not lie in throwing the baby out with the bathwater. The aim of simplifying procedural hurdles for tax officials, though a worthy one, cannot be the sole objective. Rather, it must be balanced with certain features that would prevent raids from being conducted whimsically.

Some democracies are able to achieve this balance. In the US, for instance, over decades, the SC judgments have chipped away at arbitrariness in issuing warrants, conducting raids and the like, requiring objective criteria to be demonstrated that there existed 'probable cause' as justification.

India needs similar simple, unambiguous and objective criteria to establish prima facie justification for a search and seizure. In any event, raids must be a last resort, only if there is demonstrable risk of the assessee absconding or destroying evidence.

Stipulating objective prerequisites for IT raids in India must not be convoluted. Tip-offs from predefined 'credible' sources, data algorithms to correlate expenditure and income for identifying tax fraud, and other similar measures would fit the bill. Even the routine integration of findings by the government's other, non-IT investigative agencies—instead of today's case-to-case consideration—is much needed.

Using the principles of checklist management, IT officials could be given an objective list of items to be ticked off, which would serve as a record of due process having been followed prior to a raid. Surely, the Ministry of Finance has the expertise to craft such a checklist that would pass judicial muster.

This article was first published in *The Times of India* on 15 February 2017

7

MANUFACTURING CHANGE

*For the manufacturing sector to contribute a much bigger share
in India's economy, an entirely new ecosystem is required*

In 2014, the launch of the ambitious 'Make in India' campaign to promote manufacturing in India could not have been more timely, coming as it does in the wake of the death of two iconic brands, Ambassador cars and HMT watches.

Recent years have undoubtedly seen a turnaround in India's economy, a surge in investments and optimism in the markets. However, the prevailing positive sentiment rests less on specific policy changes so far (which, till now, consist of the signalling of intent, some trial balloons and only the first few course corrections), and more on the belief that the new government means business.

Even as large investments are lined up from Japan, China and elsewhere, it is time to ensure that these (as well as domestic investments) don't get stuck in the quagmire of red tape, for which we have become infamous. India consistently fares poorly in global indices that rank countries on the basis of economic freedom, such as those by the Heritage Foundation and others. The World Bank, in its 2014 rankings on the EoDB, put India at #134 out of 189 countries.

While investments of all sorts have long had to contend with this landscape, the manufacturing sector has been especially penalized. With manufacturing contributing only 16 per cent of India's GDP—a third of China's, and far lower in absolute terms—it is clear that this sector is not pulling its weight. That means tens of millions of missing jobs for a population that desperately needs them.

Of course, it can and has been argued that India's forte is

services, while China's is manufacturing, and that we should make the most of this rather than fretting about it. Such arguments are couched in free market principles, against having an industrial policy, and in favour of letting the chips fall as they may, with each country making the most of its own competitive advantages.

There is a case for such an approach—except that India's manufacturing handicap is self-created, rather than due to any inherent shortcomings. Third World infrastructure, complex regulations, Byzantine procedures, counterproductive labour laws and a viciously extractive Inspector Raj, all contribute to disincentivizing entrepreneurship. This is especially so in manufacturing. Thus, it should be no surprise that young Indian entrepreneurs, of whom there are plenty, mostly prefer to steer clear of this sector.

Ironically, Indians have long been lauded for their entrepreneurial skills in every corner of the world, and are increasingly respected for their contributions to manufacturing on a global scale. For instance, the automotive sector has long been a benchmark of a country's manufacturing capabilities. Mahindra and Tata vehicles have been working their way up the value chain and now have significant presence in some parts of the world, as do other Indian companies in other industries.

This was a departure from an earlier era, when the likes of Lakshmi Mittal felt compelled, in the '70s, to leave India to build their empires (in his case, the world's largest steel company). However, after a few years of both domestic and foreign companies scaling up in India, recently even the best-known Indian manufacturing companies, including the Mahindras and Tatas, have been finding it far easier to grow abroad than at home.

A New Paradigm

The mood seems to be turning optimistic again, but turbocharging the manufacturing sector is going to take some doing. For starters, there are clear lessons from past efforts, which have included numerous such initiatives over the decades. From Export Oriented

Units, to Special Economic Zones, to industry-specific promotional schemes, there's nothing that has not been mooted.

Though some of these measures have experienced some success (again, the automotive industry is a good example), the share of manufacturing in the GDP has remained stagnant for decades. Typically, the poor implementation of policy thrusts is the chief villain. Take the 2011 National Manufacturing Policy, for example: a perfectly reasonable concoction, envisioning the creation of manufacturing zones with better infrastructure and updated labour laws, but not followed through on the ground. If only wishes were horses!

However, the deeper problem beyond poor policy implementation is the overall ambience of obstructionism—even hostility. Decades of statist policies were built around suspicion of trade and commerce, with the private sector being particularly tarred as exploiters. Furthermore, although the beginning of this century saw a few years of genuine entrepreneurs being lionized, political reverses, government apathy and the massive resurgence of crony capitalism saw a return to the earlier paradigm.

In the past few years, all entrepreneurs have again been viewed with suspicion for the sins of a few black sheep who conspired with rent-seekers to fleece the system. However, a country without entrepreneurs—the authentic kind, with dreams, ideas and passion— can never create enough jobs. India's entrepreneurs already have a tough time in any sector, but have bigger hurdles to overcome in the manufacturing sector, including land, labour, infrastructure, taxes, inspections and the like.

So the 'Make in India' thrust will yield results if implemented vigorously, but for the manufacturing sector to contribute a much bigger share in India's economy, an entirely new ecosystem is required. For that, a lot of undoing is needed—of accumulated laws, procedures and attitudes towards economic activity as a whole.

This article was first published in *The Times of India* on 1 October 2014

are very different now. Mandatory linkage to PAN and Aadhaar cards, but most transactions will be one of the fundamental ways to check the regeneration of black money. But the single biggest step would be to start cleaning up political funding. Some years ago, the Law Commission of India had sought public suggestions on electoral reforms, whereupon I had given written recommendations to it and to the EC. Though the Law Commission's subsequent 2015 report contained many laudable ideas for electoral transparency, its chapter on election finance reform stopped short of anything truly radical or transformative.

The most important aspect of election finance reform is that the focus around capping campaign expenses — the discussion on the legality and traceability of the money itself. Our decades-long approach focused on capping campaign expenses has not worked, and inaccurately partied money under the carpet of the election cycle. The contention that this approach and any alternative would generate — the fear that allowing higher campaign expenses would somehow undermine democracy — is misleading, and there are better ways of ensuring a level playing field than expense caps. In the event, for all practical purposes, the caps are meaningless and have only incentivised the use of unsavoury funds. The core issue is not that money buys elections, but, for high sums are introduced for electoral success. Even the own billionaire, Donald Trump's 2016 campaign reported a budget that was half of his opponent's. Rather than expense caps, it is far more important to ensure that campaign funds are traceable to a genuine source. Thus, the floor of ₹20,000, below which political contributions can be received anonymously, must be drastically lowered. This is the single greatest window of abuse, with huge sums of black money being transacted without any traceability. Though I had earlier favoured a floor of ₹5,000, I now believe it needs to be ₹1,000 or even ₹500. That would allow genuine on-the-spot donations, say, at political rallies, but make it far harder to channel large amounts of illicit funds via countless nameless donors.

Next there must be state funding to help level the playing field

FOUR

◆

FOREIGN POLICY: REDEFINING KAUTILYA'S PRINCIPLES OF REALPOLITIK

The making of the modern Indian republic was heavily influenced by an idealism that impacted both its domestic and foreign policies. This included Gandhiji's emphasis on cottage industries in an era when large industries had become the norm. It was also behind Jawaharlal Nehru's keenness to build a rapport with the world's other emerging leaders who were shaking off the shackles of colonialism.

However, to borrow a metaphor from another context, India's foreign policy often resembled 'the triumph of hope over experience'. Of course, it could be argued that most Indian freedom fighters, having cut their teeth in the domestic struggle for independence, were not actually experienced in foreign policy. There were notable exceptions like Subhas Chandra Bose, who had extensive practical experience building international alliances, but independent India was deprived of his services.

In the process, while foreign policy ought to be guided by both idealism and realpolitik, India's often had too much of the former and not enough of the latter. In fact, critics could be forgiven for seeing so much idealism in the mix as to term it naïveté instead. While seeking common cause with other underdogs of the world, India often lost sight of its own national interests.

Of course, this was not always the case, as Indira Gandhi's decisive handling of Pakistan demonstrated. But such a cool-headed approach was the exception, not the norm, as many other emotional decisions and misadventures bear witness. But starting nearly two decades after 1991, when India's economic liberalization began, there has been an evident U-turn from around the beginning of this century. Perhaps it was rekindled confidence from India gradually emerging as a key engine of the global economy after centuries. Or perhaps it was the shifting realities of geopolitics, whence our old adversaries found themselves on the same side as us and their old allies elsewhere.

But there can be no mistaking the different trajectory of Indian foreign policy from the Vajpayee era onwards, including the Manmohan Singh tenure and now, an even sharper trend of growing global influence under the energetic ministrations of Modi. This shaking off of the diffidence of earlier decades is leading India to play a role commensurate with our size, economy and contributions to global stability. And it is being broadly welcomed by nations around the world, who see India as a friendly, non-hegemonistic player.

Besides not losing sight of realpolitik, one other lesson that we, as a nation, ought to imbibe from others' foreign policy successes, is that it must be predicated on economic clout. Whether it was Great Britain in its prime, the US for over a century now, or the revamped influence that China has today, they were all based on a foundation of economic strength. Every other aspect of successful foreign policy—such as defence preparedness or building a much larger diplomatic corps—requires economic success as a prerequisite.

1

THE RAWALPINDIAN CANDIDATE

Can Pakistan's new prime minister deliver a cooling of border tensions?

The punditry following the election results in Pakistan in July 2018 has almost universally concluded that it bodes ill for any hopes of reviving India-Pakistan relations. While some in the Bollywood and cricketing circles may see signs of hope in Imran Khan's initial statements as PM-elect, realists in India have seen this movie before and are not holding their breath.

It is, nevertheless, worth taking stock of these developments. But first, a disclosure: I have visited Pakistan several times over the years and participated in many Indo-Pak Track II dialogues in both countries as well as in neutral venues. The experience has left me touched by the warm hospitality of many Pakistanis, but also sceptical about the prospects for normalcy as long as Pakistan's army retains control of its foreign policy.

What became abundantly clear over the past year is that General Headquarters (GHQ) remains addicted to its bad old ways. There was a period of hope five years ago, when the Nawaz Sharif government became the first example in Pakistan of a transfer of power from one civilian government to another. However, that was shattered once again by the army not just interfering in the government's working, but blatantly manipulating its very formation. This is not just an Indian narrative, but a global one, reflected in respectable international publications, such as *The Economist*. Thus, Khan was being modest when he fretted that Indian media had 'made him out to be a Bollywood villain'. He could justifiably claim to being portrayed negatively on a larger global canvas, though more as a proxy for the main characters.

Ironically, there was a time when Khan had taken breathtakingly out-of-the-box positions, going starkly against the Pakistani deep state orthodoxy—for instance, his 2011 statement that the Kashmir issue should be 'put on the back-burner' while Pakistan focused on its own development and cracked down on all terrorists, including those targeting India.

He was not alone. For many of the eighteen years in this century, Pakistani politicians, cutting across the spectrum, would boast that they had overcome their obsession with India. They would claim that an anti-India rhetoric had stopped figuring in their election campaigns and rue that 'such maturity was not reciprocated across the LoC'.

In private conversations, Pakistani politicians came across as pragmatic, recognizing the damage their country has suffered from decades of nurturing terrorists, and seemed open to seeking peaceful ways forward. Where we would come to a dead end in these discussions, however, was their insistence that India should commit to 'uninterrupted dialogue', irrespective of repeated terrorist attacks from bases in Pakistan.

A Ray of Hope

That the above was not reasonable to expect of Indian leaders, who faced the wrath of voters suffering from the death of near ones and destruction from Pakistan-supported terrorism, was largely lost on many Pakistani policymakers. The reason for this was their ingrained belief that India 'is just like Pakistan', that it, too, indulged in cross-border terrorism, and that India's Pakistan policy was dictated by its army in a mirror image of what happens in Pakistan.

No amount of clarifications—that India really just wants to get on with its own development, that it is not bent on harming Pakistan, that it has even tried a unilateral climbdown (as in during I.K. Gujral's prime ministership) and that despite an occasionally assertive comment by an army chief, India's Pakistan policy is most certainly not determined by him—seemed to register.

This near-schizophrenia among some Pakistani policymakers has only worsened in the past four years. There seems to be a pervasive apprehension across the LoC that PM Modi and National Security Adviser Ajit Doval are hawks who are determined to give back to Pakistan a dose of its own medicine. Such sentiments resonate with, and are exacerbated by, many Indian peaceniks.

However, this is not backed by facts. As author and South Asia specialist Myra MacDonald has tweeted, 'The deadlock (in Indo-Pak relations) came when Manmohan Singh was PM and he bent over backwards to seek a peace settlement. Modi is an excuse for Pakistan to reject peace, not the cause.' And while Modi's India has indeed resumed a muscular approach to Pakistan after decades, no one can blame him for not trying hard enough for peace.

The reality of Pakistan's internal dynamics is evident in Imran Khan's transformation. From questioning Pakistan's India policy when he was an also-ran, to now the GHQ-sponsored PM-elect, who speaks the language of the deep state, the formula for political success here is clear.

Some see a ray of hope in Khan's statements on Pakistan's desperate developmental challenges of poverty and corruption. It is distinctly reminiscent of Modi, when he exhorted Pakistanis to join hands with India to tackle these shared problems. However, Pakistan's new PM, like his predecessor, will have no wiggle room in matters related to India, without GHQ's permission.

Though Pakistan's army has, on occasion, sanctioned the cooling of border tensions, those have invariably proven to be only temporary, tactical retreats from an unwavering 'India is the existential enemy' strategy. Any real change of heart will depend entirely on external circumstances, such as Afghanistan's stability, America's resolve and, especially, China's largesse.

This article was first published in *The Times of India* on 1 August 2018

2

TRADE WARS WILL LINGER

India should concede what it must and secure what it can

As the US celebrates 242 years of its independence, the global order, which it has dominated for many decades, is again being transformed. Earlier transformations saw US influence alternately increase (such as when the Soviet Union and its satellites collapsed three decades ago) and undergo relative decline (as with its global clout vis-à-vis China in the years since the Iraq war).

The current metamorphosis is fuelled by President Donald Trump's muscular reorientation of US policies, most notably on trade. This impacts India's interests, but not necessarily in black-and-white terms. There are both pitfalls to be avoided as well as advantages to be reaped.

Though many pundits, including most American ones, have been sharply critical of the US policy shift, it is important to understand that it is not some fad foisted on the world by a whimsical leader. It was only after many months of sustained fulminations about Trump's election that more balanced opinions have started appearing, attempting to understand and explain what had earlier seemed unfathomable to liberal mainstream media.

In a major inflection, the global economic order that prevailed post World War II, including the 'consensus' on rapid globalization in recent decades, is coming unstuck. Despite the many overwhelming benefits of free trade, commitment to it, as an article of faith, meant being blind to its losers.

There indeed were losers. It is well known that countries that rebuffed market forces—preferring grossly ineffective statist and protectionist models—have, without exception, bitten the dust. The

Soviet bloc was the biggest example, and, now, countries like Cuba and Venezuela. However, there were losers even in countries that participated in and benefited from the freer global trade system.

Ironically, even in the US—the leader of this global system—there were enough disaffected voters getting a raw deal to trigger a pushback. America had seen economic woes earlier during this era too, for instance during the stagflation years of the '70s. However, productivity gains, especially from technology, had helped it rebound in the '80s and '90s.

In this century, however, with much US manufacturing having already shifted to 'cheaper labour' countries, and a dysfunctional education system, there is enormous political pressure to protect those at the bottom of the American pyramid. Of course, protectionism cannot provide a sustainable solution, with gradual pressure on competitiveness and costs, but could very well provide short- to medium-term benefits.

On the other hand, the unequivocal winners of freer trade were nations that invested in education, embraced technology, reduced red tape, and, thus, ramped up their productivity and competitiveness. Singapore is the poster child of that kind of economic trajectory, succeeding beyond all expectations. Several other countries of various sizes have experienced similar upward mobility for decades, for the same reasons.

No Winners or Losers?

India was a latecomer to the system. With its highly controlled 'mixed economy' model, it missed out on high-growth opportunities for nearly half a century after Independence. We have been catching up for the past quarter-century by gradually opening up the economy, and now with a surge in infrastructure and a substantive structural rejig—the GST. However, we are still held back by several legacy-based domestic hurdles.

Until we dismantle these hurdles, India will continue to struggle with freer trade regimes because of compulsions to be protectionist due to a lack of competitiveness. To be competitive, we need to drastically reform our anti-investment and anti-employment labour laws, speed up the judicial process, further slash red tape, reform agriculture and improve education. That would propel us into the top fifty of the EoDB Index from the current #100.

China is the outlier, having harnessed market forces and the open global trading system to grow rapidly for four decades, but is now accused of lack of reciprocal openness and of gaming the global system to secure unequal benefits. Its massive trade surpluses have spurred tensions for years and are the direct target of Trump's attempt at forceful readjustment.

China and India's responses to US tariffs are revealing. While both have retaliated, the former has blustered, ranted and threatened escalation; the latter has, wisely and quietly, done the minimum necessary.

The most significant trade war in decades, if not centuries, is now well underway. Most leaders have responded with homilies like, 'There will be only losers' (French Finance Minister, Bruno Le Maire) and 'There will be no winners' (Chinese Premier, Li Keqiang).

While these are broadly true, the harsh reality is that some have more to lose than others. It is, therefore, no coincidence that there is reportedly a sudden slowdown in Chinese funding for its Belt and Road Initiative. Moreover, China has recently shown an increased willingness to co-opt, rather than constrain, India through economic overtures. For its part, having demonstrated resolve during the Doklam standoff last year, India has now responded positively.

In discussions for creating the world's largest trading bloc, the Regional Comprehensive Economic Partnership, India sought the free movement of people in lieu of lowering tariffs. That is a big ask amid growing global concern about immigration. However, India will need some such sweetener, perhaps capped in absolute numbers for a specified period, until its economic competitiveness is improved with further domestic reform.

This article was first published in *The Times of India* on 4 July 2018

3

GENTRIFY THE NEIGHBOURHOOD

*For India, a double-digit growth can be the best
foreign policy option of all*

Even its worst critics admit, if only in private, that the one area where the Modi government has undoubtedly shone is in foreign policy. Moreover, those who take political potshots at the PM's travels abroad, ironically also claim credit (with some justification), for the origin of many of his diplomatic initiatives. In any event, it is difficult to ignore that the world sees India far more favourably than it did in 2014.

The last time there was such a turnaround in India's global image was at the turn of the century, against the backdrop of sanctions after the 1998 nuclear test. Then, as now, the world overcame its reservations not just because of our stellar record against nuclear proliferation, but clearly also because of India's growing economic clout.

One aspect of that earlier turnaround, which holds lessons for this one, is the hubris that took hold of our policymaking. Hubris about our economy—that we were somehow destined to be the next economic superpower, irrespective of whether we nurtured or damaged that prospect—was years in the making. But, hubris about breaking free from the constraints of dealing with our South Asian neighbours was there all along.

For decades, India had been held back not only by its own blinkered economic policies, but also by frictions in the subcontinent that ranged from the petty to the existential. The yearning to be done with recalcitrant neighbours—have-nots like us, but who seemed unwilling or unable to leave the past behind, and join the twenty-first-century global mainstream—was understandable. However, it wasn't practical. Unlike aspirational and upwardly mobile families who can simply up and leave for a better neighbourhood, nations have geographical limitations.

This time around, India has clearly recognized that to achieve our overall potential, we need to do more to gentrify the neighbourhood. This has been evident from the first days of this government, beginning with the precedent-setting invitation to South Asian heads of government to attend the swearing in.

Symbolism is important, and the PM has done more than his fair share of sending out the right signals. However, resetting decades of hardened positions requires more than symbolism, and it is heartening to see that realpolitik is finally taking hold.

Take, for instance, the principle of 'non-reciprocity', which acknowledges India's huge size relative to other South Asian nations, and concludes that it needs to do more than just seek quid pro quo from them. Some form of this has existed for long, most notably in the so-called 'Gujral doctrine' of the late '90s. However, while that included elements of a unilateral drawing down of strategic assets, the Modi doctrine is closer to Teddy Roosevelt's 'speak softly, and carry a big stick'.

Two-speed Policy

India, whose economy is a startling 82 per cent of all the South Asian Association for Regional Cooperation countries, is now loosening its purse strings for neighbours, even as it begins a much overdue beefing up of defence capabilities. A flurry of India-assisted projects has been announced recently in many South Asian countries, including railways, hydropower, transmission lines and the like. Many others, as well as policy changes to help integrate their economies with India's, are on the anvil. Underpinning all this is the growing realization that double-digit economic growth is likely the best foreign policy of all.

Admittedly, some of this had been initiated prior to the Modi government, by the UPA (or even earlier). Though there are some new proposals as well, the most important feature now is the refreshing urgency that pervades India's foreign policy establishment. In no small measure, this is enhanced by the quiet efficiency of the foreign minister, as well as an accomplished foreign secretary who is to the manner born.

Just as important as any of this, of course, is the cooperation of Opposition parties. Though foreign policy has never been a major source of discord in India, it is, nevertheless, a fact that lack of consensus in the recent past had led to delays on crucial initiatives, such as the now-concluded Bangladesh land accord.

In recent years, our relationship with Bangladesh has epitomized the turnaround in South Asia that India has been seeking. Its crackdown on radicalism at home, as well as action against terrorist groups using its territory as safe havens to target India, has brought a welcome transformation on our eastern front. Thus, while PM Modi's visits to other South Asian countries have also been hugely successful, it is fitting that the first truly epoch-making breakthrough is with Bangladesh.

In this new orchestra of feel-good South Asian music, the only discordant note relates to Pakistan. Despite the same initial outreach as with other neighbours, India's hope for rapprochement with its western neighbour remains mired in Pakistan's atavistic fears and instincts. The same old script of border provocations, shelter to 'non-State actors', and intransigence on trade, both bilateral and regional, keeps playing out over and over again.

For the first time, however, the rest of South Asia is no longer content to wait until the weakest link in the chain is strengthened. India has, thus, settled on a two-speed policy—that is, full speed ahead with all neighbours, including Pakistan, preferably, but without, if necessary.

This article was first published in *The Times of India* on 10 June 2015

4

INTERNATIONALIZE PAK VILLAINY

Kautilya's principles of realpolitik must replace idealism in India's Pakistan policy

Visiting Washington DC in September 2016 with a delegation of Indian MPs, it was astonishing to note how far that nation has gone in recognizing Pakistan for what it is. Large numbers of US government officials, Congressmen, senators, former presidential candidates and others are speaking bluntly about Pakistan.

In a far cry from its 2004 designation as a 'major non-NATO (North Atlantic Treaty Organization) ally', many American politicians now unhesitatingly call Pakistan a duplicitous rogue State that uses terrorism as a tool of its foreign policy. While acknowledging that Pakistan has cracked down on some terrorist organizations, they lambast it for continuing to shelter those like the Haqqani network, Lashkar-e-Taiba and Jaish-e-Mohammed (JeM), which target American, Afghan and Indian interests.

Several US lawmakers have gone beyond words and have taken steps to rein in Pakistan, such as by stalling US defence assistance. Other legislative manoeuvres aim to help India access restricted defence technologies. These are motivated by India's economic growth, the influence of its successful diaspora, mutual interests and concerns about China.

Yet, it is far from clear whether a pivotal moment has arrived to successfully isolate Pakistan in the eyes of the civilized world. As pointed out by Ata Hasnain, a retired Indian general and respected commentator, Pakistan's impunity stems from its uniquely strategic geography. It has leveraged that to entice, flirt with, and blackmail the world's leading powers into tolerating its bad behaviour.

Nevertheless, many observers have concluded that India should now unhesitatingly internationalize Pakistan's villainy. For years, India has been diffident about doing so, for fear of playing into the hands of Pakistan, which has been trying to re-internationalize the Kashmir issue, despite the Shimla agreement to keep it bilateral.

However, 2018 is very different from 1989, when Pakistan reneged on its Shimla commitment and turned the heat on Kashmir. Now, it is amply clear that while most of the world has no interest in getting involved in India and Pakistan's Kashmir dispute (unless war in the subcontinent is imminent), terrorism is another matter altogether.

The 'root cause' theory—of terrorism being fostered by political circumstances—has lost enormous ground in recent years. Moreover, battered by a summer of ghastly jihadi terror attacks, the rest of the world now has far more empathy for India.

In any event, India has to break out of the box it has been in since 1998, when Pakistan redefined the meaning of nuclear deterrence. Traditionally, the cold war dynamic of nuclear-armed adversaries resulted in mutual restraint, lest any provocation get out of hand, leading to the ultimate 'mutually assured destruction (MAD)*'. However, Pakistan has used its nuclear cover quite differently, by continually attacking India through its proxies, counting on our unilateral 'strategic restraint'.

Carrots Alone Don't Work

After the usual lack of any immediate military response to Uri, Pakistan may again be feeling that its stratagem is justified. But that would be a mistake. Unilateral strategic restraint has had two main objectives for India: prevent Pakistan from re-internationalizing the Kashmir dispute, and stay focused on our own economic growth,

---

*MAD is a doctrine of military strategy in which a full-scale usage of nuclear weapons between two or more warring nations would lead to a mutual, assured and complete annihilation.

rather than scare investments away with tit-for-tat jousting with an unstable neighbour.

The first is much less a concern now, but the second remains a constraint. Thus, PM Modi's speech in Kozhikode in 2016 was yet another example of India taking the high road. It was reminiscent of George Bernard Shaw's famous quip to 'Never wrestle with a pig. You get dirty, and besides, the pig likes it.'

More such messaging is necessary, aimed at the Pakistani people rather than their leadership, but will not be sufficient. It is worth trying to undo the Pakistani State's brainwashing of its people about their own history and the vastly exaggerated threat from India, but that cannot be our only response. So, how can India break out of strategic gridlock?

South Asia experts, like author and academic Christine Fair, argue that India should leverage its new clout with the US and reach out to other major actors like China to obtain UN sanctions to ring fence terrorists operating from Pakistan. This is good advice, and to some extent, is already being attempted, but it cannot yield quick results and likely won't be enough to eliminate terrorist attacks altogether.

Ironically, it takes a former Pakistani journalist and diplomat to articulate what few Indian or American policy wonks are willing to say bluntly. Husain Haqqani, a former Pakistani ambassador to the US and now a think tank scholar and prolific author, had this to say a few days before the Uri attack: 'It seems Pakistan's establishment will not stop using terrorism unless it pays a higher price for it than Pakistan is already paying.'

For a country with the Ashoka Stambh as its national emblem, it has taken India far too long to recollect Kautilya's mantra of statecraft: *sama, dana, bheda, danda* (conciliate, compensate, divide, fight). However, there are clear indications that India has now finally understood that carrots alone don't work, and sometimes sticks are necessary too.

There is unexplored headroom between responding to every terrorist attack with only words of condemnation, and the other extreme of triggering cycles of escalation, leading to war. Realpolitik, not utopian principles, should guide this exploration. Covert operations, Balochistan, Indus Waters and other unthought-of options must all be on the table.

This article was first published in *The Times of India* on 28 September 2016

5

A WHIFF OF DETENTE

'India bashing' matters less in Pakistani politics,
but remains the mainstay of its foreign policy

Post Pathankot, there was something different about the rigmarole of India's engagement with Pakistan, but that phase seems to have run out of steam. By all accounts, the relationship is back to its pathetic old 'normal', or perilously close to it. So, was it just déjà vu all over again—yet another Indian PM's naiveté being exploited one more time by the other side?

Not exactly.

What was new was in what was missing: instant blame and defensiveness. India did not, as is usual, jump to blame Pakistan, but methodically traced the attack back to the jihadi terror group, JeM; neither did Pakistan instantly disclaim any involvement, and in fact, rather stunningly, also corroborated the link back to JeM. Although that was later withdrawn, contrast it with Pakistan's long obfuscation on captured Mumbai attacker Ajmal Kaṣab.

There was another aspect that was new. Even during the Track II dialogues, which are supposed to foster candour, Pakistani participants would, in the past, be defensive about their country's links to terror. Any discussion on Pakistani links to attacks on the Indian embassy in Afghanistan, for instance, would be pooh-poohed. Moreover, links between Pakistan's deep state and terrorist outfits would be dismissed as being in the distant past, followed by the now routine 'Pakistan is the biggest victim of terror' dodge.

However, at a Track II dialogue in April 2016, there was a refreshing difference. Rather than being dismissive or defensive about Pakistani links to the Pathankot attack, there was indeed the hoped-for candour. It struck some Indian interlocutors that, this time, their Pakistani counterparts, instead of just papering over their military's contradictory interests, were far more open to acknowledging the facts on cross-border terrorism, and perhaps even cooperating with India against this scourge.

Now, it appears that all that was too good to be true; but of course, many say that this should have been expected. The Pakistani deep state perfidies are not new, and India should have kept in mind the betrayals of Kargil, Mumbai and many others that have followed every new initiative.

The resistance by Pakistan's deep state to any real breakthrough with India can be understood from the cliché that while most countries own an army, in Pakistan, it is the army that owns a country. Tellingly, the UK newspaper *The Guardian* cited Pakistani author Ayesha Siddiqa on how 'Five giant conglomerates, known as "welfare foundations", run thousands of businesses... (including) military-run bakeries, banks, insurance companies, and universities.'

According to South Asia-expert Kathryn Alexeeff, 'Pakistan's military has extensive economic power... this has numerous negative implications, not least of which is that it makes long-term successful economic reforms nearly impossible.' Therein lies the crux of the problem, holding Pakistan back from the goals of peace, growth and prosperity, which would inevitably and drastically curtail the military's dominance.

Though some have suggested that India should, therefore, bypass Pakistan's civilian government and directly build a bridge with its military, it has never been accepted by India. And rightly so, for the fundamental disconnect is not between India and Pakistan's interests, but between India and the Pakistan's militaries.

Two Steps Forward, and One Back

Pakistan's fragile democracy growing stronger roots is as much in India's interest as Pakistan's. And now, a few years after Pakistan's first ever transfer of power through elections from one civilian government to another, is not the time to change tack on that core philosophy. 'India bashing' has progressively mattered less and less in Pakistani elections and politics, but continues to be the bulwark of its defence and foreign policies, ultimately determined by you-know-who.

The evident rapport between PMs Narendra Modi and Nawaz Sharif was disconcerting to Pakistan's deep state, just as similar, earlier bonhomie between Vajpayee and Sharif had been. As Pathankot inevitably followed Modi's visit to Lahore, the still enduring entente, with a Pakistani team visiting Pathankot, had to be disrupted perforce—thus, the melodramatic arrest of an alleged Indian spy.

All nations gather intelligence, but the Pakistani military has consistently tried to portray a false equivalence between its active support of cross-border Jihadi terror groups and India's far more traditional intelligence activities.

As Pakistani journalist Cyril Almeida has written on the spy saga, 'The audience was internal... The boys are talking to us... "Pakistan, we're on your side and we need you on ours".'

In all this, China's stymying of a UN resolution naming JeM chief Masood Azhar as a wanted terrorist was par for the course. Subsequently, Azhar has reportedly criticized Sharif but praised China, which is indicative of the struggle within Pakistan between the military and the civilians. That China uses Pakistan as a cheap option to act as a drag on India's rise, is no secret, and this is something that must continue to guide our strategic thinking.

Clearly, the new normal was short-lived. Nonetheless, there was more to it than mere déjà vu. The decades-old script was altered, even if briefly, which means that it is not forever unalterable. In fact, even as this is being written, the two PMs have yet again picked up the phone to commiserate on the latest tragedies in each other's country. On balance, these past few months have seen the proverbial two steps forward, and one back.

This article was first published in *The Times of India* on 11 May 2016

6

JOINING THE BIG BOYS

The United Nations Security Council permanent membership should remain a key foreign policy goal for India, but not the pre-eminent one

'The future isn't what it used to be' is one of the many aphorisms attributed to Yogi Berra, a great American baseball player of the '50s, who passed away in 2015. He might as well have been talking about the conundrums that the UN faces today, especially about its Security Council that India aspires to join as a permanent member.

Time was when the vaunted UN Security Council (UNSC) was the Cold War club, where the big boys played, keeping the world secure. Despite their great rivalries, they would prevent an assassination here, or a regime change there, from escalating into something more disastrous on a global scale. But the world today is a very different place, and the UNSC's ability to impose or restore order is far more limited.

Just a quick glance at the situation in Ukraine and Syria shows that the inability of the five permanent members to agree on key challenges—let alone solutions—is crippling this once powerful body. The nature of threats itself, which challenge the world order, has evolved—growing from just nuclear concerns, to non-State terror groups, mass migrations, climate change and a looming water crisis.

However, the UNSC still has relevance, particularly in dealing with traditional nation state nuclear threats that are so far beyond the pale that they cannot be ignored. Thus, the squabbling permanent members—be they former, present or upcoming superpowers—have felt compelled to work together on the emergence of Iran and North Korea as nuclear States.

It is in this context that India's aim to be a permanent member of the UNSC is still significant. In fact, apart from India's growing importance in economic terms, it is ever odder for the world's largest democracy, projected to be the most populous nation by 2022, to not be part of such decision-making. Today, the UN, with 193 member countries, faces vastly different challenges than it did when it started seventy years ago, with fifty-one members.

In 2015, the UN accepted, by consensus, a text laying out the framework for discussing a UNSC reform. Though opinions vary on whether this reflects a significant breakthrough or only a technical one, it is, nevertheless, a move beyond the 'having discussions about how to have discussions' stage.

Despite this progress, it is unlikely that a reform will happen quickly. In any case, it has been widely reported that this breakthrough, which India considers is in its interest, was opposed by some countries, including the usual suspects, Pakistan and China, and even Italy. What should be even more revealing is the apparent lack of support from old ally Russia and even the US, which has otherwise overtly supported India's case for being part of a restructured Security Council.

Of course, China has been a UNSC permanent member from the beginning, when India had supported its cause, but that is no reason to expect reciprocity. All nations act from their perceptions of their own national interest, and so will China and India in the present circumstances.

Developing Economic Clout

Thus, it is appropriate that India is hedging its bets by working towards memberships of other multilateral groupings and agencies. These include a founding role in new economic institutions like the so-called BRICS Bank (established by the BRICS States of Brazil, Russia, India, China and South Africa) and the Asian Infrastructure Investment Bank. India has also been gradually getting more involved in existing groupings, both economic and strategic, such as the Association of Southeast Asian Nations, and the Shanghai Cooperation Organisation. Similarly, it is finally getting serious about a role in the Internet Corporation for Assigned Names and Numbers, the key internet administrative agency.

In addition, it is illustrative to examine the path taken by China over the past thirty-five years, during which it transitioned from being approximately at par with India in per capita income, to becoming the world's second-largest economy, five times that of India's. In recent years, China has used its new economic clout to win friends and influence countries through developmental assistance.

In fact, it has rapidly overtaken Western nations in the amounts it sanctions for such purposes, dovetailed with its own future mercantile and strategic interests. Though India's growth trajectory has been shallower, it has, nevertheless, also started yielding similar manoeuvring room in foreign policy.

India's ongoing transition from a purely developing nation into one that is an aspirational middle-income country, capable of extending aid to others, became apparent a decade ago during the Indian Ocean tsunami and other subsequent natural disasters. By 2012, India had formalized its overseas aid efforts by setting up the Development Partnership Administration (DPA) within the Ministry of External Affairs.

In 2013–14, the DPA had an annual budget of more than a billion dollars, and since then, has scaled up its ambitions even more. PM Modi has been a key driver of this, keeping up a frenetic globetrotting schedule in an effort to make up for lost time. His recent announcements of DPA assistance include projects worth $2 billion in Bangladesh, and $1 billion each in Nepal and Mongolia, among many others.

In this evolving scenario, the UNSC permanent membership should remain a key foreign policy goal for India, but not the pre-eminent one. Moreover, every aspect of India's foreign policy, including this, would benefit immensely from faster economic growth.

This article was first published in *The Times of India* on 30 September 2015

---◆---

FIVE

LAW: JUSTICE FOR ALL

On becoming independent, India decided to essentially retain the systems and structures of the British Raj. Oh sure, we enacted a constitution giving equal rights to all citizens, but, unlike the Americans for instance, we retained colonial structures like the civil service, the police, the courts, the proto-parliament (which had been in place for a few decades), and the accumulated statutes and laws.

With every passing year, it becomes evermore clear that we have done ourselves a disservice. For one, the governance structures of colonial India had not primarily been designed in the interest of the people, but to enable control. In any case, most of these structures were adaptations of what existed in nineteenth century Britain, which the UK has, in many cases, overhauled drastically.

Our democracy needs some burnishing to be better adapted for the modern world. The most important would be to replace arbitrariness with reasoned and rule-based procedures, and to introduce checks and balances in a manner that the government is neither so unquestioned that it becomes autocratic, nor so handicapped that governance comes to a halt.

Whether it is the procedures to deal with mercy petitions on death sentences, or the unlimited number of adjournments in the courts that cause litigation to linger for decades, Indians deserve better than the subjectivity that reigns at present. And for appointments to key statutory and constitutional posts, neither should the government, with a mandate, be devoid of any role, nor should they have unbridled power to make such appointments just because they have a majority.

The principle of checks and balances between the various pillars of governance is an important aspect of democracy, but is still very much a work-in-progress in the largest democracy of the world. This also applies to the array of rights and protections that have been extended to vulnerable sections. Some of the most controversial debates of the day are essentially a tussle between the fundamentals of due process on the one hand, which every free society ought to guarantee its citizens, and the frustrations with a clogged justice system that is unable to deliver justice swiftly.

Another key aspect of this section deals with the conflict between the individual rights that our Constitution guarantees every citizen, and certain group rights that have long been embedded in our laws. In the immediate aftermath of the independence and partition, the necessary legislation and implementation of several hard decisions, though ensconced in the Constitution as desirable, had been put off for another day. After seven decades, at least some of these touchy issues need to be confronted and a consensus evolved.

Finally, an important theme discussed in this section is the need to deal with rapidly evolving technology, its benefits and downsides, and how regulatory regimes need to adapt to the changing scenario. Concerns about privacy are genuine and are a burning issue of modern times. Technologies like biometrics have enormous potential to do good—for instance, by drastically reducing fraud and corruption by deduplicating multiple fake identities. At the same time, there are risks associated with such technologies that need to be mitigated and tightly controlled through appropriate regulation.

1

THE YAKUB MEMON FRENZY

*Clear, time-bound procedures will end unnecessary
controversy over executions*

In 2015, the frenzied discourse in the weeks leading up to, and even after, the execution of Yakub Memon saw different narratives being conflated, resulting in much confusion, frustration, anger and bitterness on all sides. Take the arguments by those against the death penalty in principle.

Indians in this category are not alone, and, in fact, echo views shared by millions across the world, most commonly in many modern, democratic nations. In recent years, American opponents of the death penalty have had their stand vindicated by many US death row convicts who have subsequently been exonerated by new scientific breakthroughs, such as the latest DNA testing methods.

This view deserves respect, and it is important to note that subscribing to it does not automatically make someone unpatriotic or soft on terrorism. It is undoubtedly time for a sustained national debate on this topic, rather than only occasionally, when there is an execution. However, the rightful place for that debate is in public and in the Parliament. As long as the law provides for the death penalty, it is useless—even damaging—to drag courts into it.

It was particularly galling for many, when this debate reached a fever pitch on behalf of someone like Memon, and many commentators got their vocabulary mixed up, not to mention their logic.

Many anti-death penalty advocates strayed from the core principles of objecting to any execution, into defending a particularly heinous individual on specious grounds. Instead of treating the mercy petition as just that, some got caught up in arguing the merits of a conviction that had taken two decades and been settled by the SC itself.

Memon was not some innocent, who somehow got caught up in a bad situation. The principle that his guilt must be established beyond a reasonable doubt was met by the SC, which observed that the evidence 'amply proved his involvement' in arranging to receive ammunitions, conducting surveys, choosing targets, and loading vehicles with RDX. Moreover, the SC's own guideline that the death penalty must only be given in the rarest of rare cases was surely applicable to a key perpetrator of the Mumbai bombings, which killed 257 people and injured 713.

India's excruciatingly slow judicial system and low conviction rates have led to much resentment. When there seems to be no end in sight even after a rare conviction, in such horrific cases, the anger boils over. Further, with convicted terrorists, there is an extra degree of angst about simply incarcerating them, with apprehensions that this could be an incentive for further acts of terror, especially hijackings aimed at getting them released.

Hobbled by Ambiguity and Discretion

The conflated narratives on Memon went beyond mixing up the plea for mercy with poorly argued critiques of the legal process. Many who conceded his guilt and the legitimacy of his conviction, nevertheless tried to make a case other than that of mercy for commuting the death sentence. They also argued the mitigating circumstances or alleged discrimination against Muslim death row convicts.

The allusion that Memon had turned approver and was subsequently ditched by the Indian establishment, always seemed a bit of an afterthought and, in any case, rested on weak ground. The facts are murky, but a careful scrutiny of reportage is revealing. He may well have been lured out of Pakistan, along with evidence incriminating the Inter-Services Intelligence and Dawood Ibrahim, and hope of striking a deal as an approver. However, midway in Nepal, he clearly did not like what was on offer, and was headed back when he was apprehended.

The claim, rebutted by his supporters, of Memon being found wandering in Delhi's railway station was more than likely a bit of legal fiction, intended to overcome the awkwardness of an unofficial extradition across the Nepal-India border. However, that, by itself, is much ado about nothing consequential. The crucial issue is that, finally, there seems to have been no agreement for seeking a lesser sentence in lieu of cooperation, and neither does that seem to have been claimed during the trial.

The allegation that Muslim death row convicts are being discriminated against is worrisome and deserves close examination. It is true that following political uproars, one Sikh and three Tamil death row convicts had their sentences commuted to life imprisonment in 2014. The SC, citing inordinate delay by the government in processing their mercy petitions, had done this.

However, it did exactly the same, also in 2014, in the case of one Jafar Ali, convicted of murdering his wife and five daughters, which clearly refutes the 'Muslim discrimination' angle. Dragging in the case of Afzal Guru, hanged in 2013, is illogical, since it predates the SC ruling on the principle of inordinate delay. Equally illogical was any expectation that the President, having once rejected a mercy petition for Memon filed by his brother, ought to drag out the decision on a second plea.

Nevertheless, the Memon saga showed that India's handling of death row convicts is hobbled by ambiguity and discretion, such as how long mercy petitions can linger on. This is a recipe for abuse, both by convicts gaming the system with multiple and overlapping appeals, as well as by politicians responding to sectional sentiments.

Reform is essential, especially the introduction of clear, time-bound procedures.

This article was first published in *The Times of India* on 5 August 2015

2

THE COLLEGIUM HAS RUN ITS COURSE

Even in the new National Judicial Appointments Commission system, the judiciary has effective veto on appointing judges

India is the only country in the world where the higher judiciary is self-appointed—that is, the existing judges appoint new ones. This so-called 'collegium system' has been in place since 1993, based on three SC judgments in 1981, 1993 and 1998, together known as the 'Three Judges Cases'.

The Constitution does not provide for such a collegium, and judges used to be appointed by the executive branch—that is, the government—until 1993. However, the Constitution not only guarantees an independent judiciary, but also specifically mandates the SC to interpret the Constitution itself. Thus, it is particularly important to understand the backdrop to the highest court's interpretation that judicial independence could only be ensured through such a unique system.

Well before the first judgment in 1981, rumblings of discontent had emerged against what were seen as Indira Gandhi's efforts to establish the executive's primacy over the judiciary. For instance, the highly regarded Justice Hans Raj Khanna's resignation on being superseded to the chief justice's post in January 1977 had resulted in weeks of protests by bar associations across the country.

Now, after a constitutional amendment has finally created the much-discussed NJAC, the matter has come full circle, with the SC hearing a public interest litigation (PIL) against it. Though the collegium system solved the original problem it was intended to tackle—the executive's whimsical appointment of judges—it has led to unanticipated new problems.

Amid whispered allegations of favouritism, nepotism, groupism and outright bias, the collegium system has also resulted in a significant number of vacancies in the higher judiciary—10 per cent in the SC and 36 per cent in the HCs—even as they collectively grapple with a mammoth load of more than 5 million cases.

Every now and then, someone bemoans India's abysmally low ratio of judges to a population of 13 per million, versus 50–100 in Western democracies. Among others, the Law Commission and several chief justices have made recommendations to dramatically increase the number of judgeships at all levels. The easy excuse for the executive and legislative branches for not acting on this is that even existing posts in the higher judiciary don't get filled up.

Besides accusations of bias and inefficiency, the collegium system does not even meet the basic standards of transparency expected of the high office. Among many credible critics, retired SC Justice Ruma Pal has called its workings 'the best-kept secret in the country'. Finally, and perhaps most importantly, the collegium goes against the principle of checks and balances crucial to every democracy.

In Sync with Changing Times

True, judges can be impeached by the Parliament, but that is extremely rare and in fact, despite calls for it on several occasions, has happened only once. In any case, impeachment is akin to the Parliament's own 'nuclear option' of a no-confidence vote: necessary as a last resort, when no other option exists, but hardly suitable as a means to facilitate routine functions. Just as the Parliament is in desperate need of reforms to unclog its day-to-day functioning, so is the judiciary. In such issues concerning the fundamental tenets of constitutional democracy, it is instructive to examine the practices of other countries. A quick glance at how other democracies appoint judges of the higher judiciary is revealing. They run the gamut, from the executive branch having sole authority, to having some role for the legislature, but only rarely is the judiciary itself involved.

In Canada, for example, a screening committee of MPs shortlists names, from which the PM makes the final selection. In the US, only the president can nominate names, but they must, then, be approved by the Senate. In Japan, it is the cabinet's decision. There is no country—and especially not any respectable democracy—which has a totally self-appointing system like India's collegium.

Perhaps most telling is the case of the UK, particularly because of the shared roots of our political systems. There, judges used to be appointed by the lord chancellor, a member of the cabinet. However, after a 2005 constitutional amendment, a Judicial Appointments Commission (JAC) was set up for the purpose. Strikingly, not only is the UK's JAC not headed by a judge and only a third of its members are judges, but another third are required to be laypersons without a legal background!

By contrast, India's NJAC is headed by the chief justice, and half its members are judges of the SC. Another third of its members are persons of eminence, selected by a panel consisting of the chief justice, the PM, and the leader of the largest Opposition party. Thus, while introducing checks and balances, the NJAC, nevertheless, gives India's judiciary the most say, compared to any other country. In fact, the judiciary effectively still gets a veto over appointments.

In retrospect, the events of the '70s and '80s justified the SC taking unto itself the appointment of judges, in the interest of keeping the judiciary independent. However, times have changed. The judiciary's independence is no longer in doubt, and India is a much more mature democracy, whose citizens deserve better. It is time for the highest court to loosen its grip a little, and let the pendulum, which has been going from one extreme to the other, rest in the middle.

This article was first published in *The Times of India* on 13 May 2015

3

HOW TO TACKLE RUNAWAY CRIME

The Talwars's trial paints a grim picture of a broken criminal justice system in desperate need of reform

India's broken criminal justice system was exemplified by the long-running trial of a dentist couple, the Talwars, whom the Allahabad HC recently acquitted of murdering their teenage daughter nearly a decade ago. From investigations with contradictory conclusions, to incompetence in preserving basic evidence, to crucial documents not being filed in court, and staggering delays—this case had it all.

Add to that the HC's scathing observation that the lower court judge, who had earlier found the Talwars guilty, was 'unmindful of the basic tenets of law', and a grim picture emerges of the state of affairs. It is even grimmer for the millions of other cases that do not dominate the news.

Occasionally, when horrific cases like the Nirbhaya gang rape and murder straddle the news cycle for more than the customary day or two, public outrage compels governments to fast-track the investigation and prosecution. However, there is a long overdue—and now desperate—need for systemic reforms.

Statistics corroborate the widespread belief that our fight against crime is inadequate. Even after adjusting for increasing population, India's crime rate has been rising over the years. The decade from 2005 to 2015 saw a 28 per cent increase in complaints of cognizable offences, from 450 per lakh population, to 580.

Using similar measures for the resources needed, the vast shortage of police, judges, etc., is stark. Against a UN norm of 222 police personnel per lakh of population, India's officially sanctioned strength is a paltry 181, and the actual strength is an abysmal 137. Similarly, all the judges in the country now add up to just eighteen per million population, despite a three-decades old Law Commission recommendation to increase it to fifty, which itself is at the low-end of the ratio in developed countries.

There are also enormous shortfalls in the number of police stations, weapons, forensic science laboratories and the like. Consider just forensics: nearly a million items sent for forensic examination in India—representing a shocking 38 per cent of all such cases—remain unattended for a year or more. The effect of that on investigations of lakhs of crimes is nothing short of cruel.

However, the problem is not just of numbers, it is equally about processes and structures. Three crucial areas for reform are interminable court delays, ineffective prosecutions and outdated police service rules.

Overhaul Our Criminal Justice System

Many chief justices of India have pleaded for courts to enforce a maximum of three adjournments per case, but in vain. Delays have become hardwired in the culture of our judiciary. The Vajpayee government tried a go-around by launching fast track courts with expedited procedures. Those succeeded, with a resolution rate far higher than existing courts.

However, when the Union government discontinued funding in 2011, few states picked up the tab to keep them going. Thankfully, following the 14th Finance Commission's recommendations, Delhi has now again allocated more than ₹4,100 crore to set up 1,800 new fast track courts. These funds are available till 2020, but the onus remains on state governments to avail of them.

Similarly, though the SC's recent decision to make public the deliberations of its secretive 'collegium' system of appointing judges is welcome, it, nevertheless, disappointingly remains the world's only self-appointing judiciary.

The SC's 2015 judgment overruling the NJAC, passed unanimously by the Parliament, was a huge setback to the process of streamlining and introducing checks and balances in judicial appointments. Though modelled on the UK's excellent JAC, where judges have a lesser say in appointing judges, the Indian version provided far more powers to the judiciary.

In fact, the NJAC composition had effectively given a veto to the SC in appointing judges, while making the process more transparent and broad-based.

Regarding prosecutions, India's conviction rate of 47 per cent—compared to more than 85 per cent in developed democracies like France, Japan and the US—exposes the gross inadequacies of our system. I have advocated, in a private members' bill in the Lok Sabha, for an independent directorate of prosecutions in every state. These would report directly to the state home department, with stipulated objective criteria on caseloads and pendency. Furthermore, to reward capability rather than political connections, appointments of prosecutors from district level upwards should have checks and balances, with concurrence by the judiciary.

Finally, much has been written about insulating the police from political interference, with recommendations such as fixed tenures to prevent frequent transfers. Many of those ideas are excellent and must be implemented, but beyond a point, they will be contrary to the spirit of democracy if the police are not accountable to the elected polity. Equal emphasis must be put, as in other modern democracies, on devolving some routine police functions to district and even panchayat levels. States like Assam and Kerala have launched community policing initiatives that bear watching.

The first requirement of a republic must be to maintain law and order, and provide relatively swift justice to its citizenry. Our polity has often put off important reforms because they do not pay off in time for the next election cycle. However, the need to overhaul our criminal justice system has reached a volatile tipping point that must no longer be ignored.

This article was first published in *The Times of India* on 25 October 2017

4

IS PUNJAB FOLLOWING PAKISTAN?

Many Indians, who identify as 'secular', are fighting for a fifteenth-century version of it

The attempt by Punjab's governing party to legislate an anti-blasphemy law has attracted criticism, as a step backward from a modern, democratic, secular republic. This comes after a prominent MP of the same party accused its opponents in the Union government of turning India 'into a Hindu Pakistan'.

The irony, of course, is that Pakistan is among a handful of theistic States with strong anti-blasphemy laws. There lies the crux of India's long-running schism on secularism: even those who swear by it, have no compunction in blatantly flouting its basic tenets. This is because the debate has long ago forsaken any rational discourse on ideas or principles, and simply become an 'us versus them' exercise in virtue-signalling—and, of course, consolidating votes.

To be fair, an anti-blasphemy law has existed in India since the charged atmosphere of Hindu-Muslim tensions in the '20s, with punishment for 'malicious acts intended to outrage religious feelings'. This new bill in Punjab (after a previous one against vandalizing the Guru Granth Sahib was returned by the Union government last year) is 'more secular' in that it criminalizes vandalism against holy books of four religions.

Thus, this new draft of the Bill comes closer to what has come to be the Indian version of secularism, as propagated by self-avowed secularists. This version exhorts the State to engage with, and respect, all religions' practices.

However, that is not what secularism classically meant, and still means, in most developed democracies: to treat religion strictly as a private matter and keep Church and State separate. That is, the State ought not to have views on any religion's beliefs and practices, and should be guided solely by constitutional tenets.

A key aspect of classical secularism was its co-development and strong linkage with classical liberalism. In contrast with what modern liberalism is increasingly morphing into, its classical origins emphasized not just secularism, but also freedom of speech and, crucially, the rights of individuals rather than those of the tribes, clans, groups or religions to which they belonged.

In a Bind

In moving away from classical secularism, like their global compatriots, many Indian liberals have also gradually compromised those two other linked principles mentioned above. In fact, the '20s anti-blasphemy law was incorporated by the Raj in reaction to a pamphlet critical of Islam's prophet, leading, in the '50s, to the 'reasonable restrictions' clause on free speech.

Similarly, many liberals have shown themselves less committed to individual rights, even as they champion the rights of disenfranchised groups, such as caste or religious minorities. Of course, championing the rights of groups facing discrimination is laudable; where it is less so, is when the rights of individuals within those groups are treated as subservient to group rights. That also violates the Constitution, which grants equal rights to each individual citizen.

The textbook example of this dichotomy is on the issue of triple talaq. Many of the same activists, who take up cudgels against discrimination faced by Muslims and women, falter when it comes to the individual constitutional rights of women who happen to be Muslim.

The problem with what passes for secularism in India is that it brings discretion and interpretation into the equation. Why, for instance, are Hindu temples administered by the government when all other religious communities manage their own places of worship? And, if the Punjab bill becomes law, will vandalizing holy books beyond the four listed in it, not be criminal? What if you or I founded a new religion and wrote new holy books, as we are entitled to by the Constitution?

Ultimately, to be truly secular, a modern democracy has no real alternative to keeping the State out of religion. Otherwise, it must settle for an earlier, lesser standard of secularism as practised in, say, the Ottoman Empire. There, the State religion was Islam but minorities were tolerated and enjoyed certain protections. They were even allowed their own laws within their communities, unless conflicts spilled over beyond their neighbourhoods. However, there was no question of all its citizens enjoying equal protection under the law.

Indian secularism is caught in a bind. On the one hand, our Constitution supports the modern standard for it, and is backed by millennia of secular culture, such as the religious freedoms guaranteed by Emperor Ashoka. Yet, many Indians who identify as secular are fighting for a fifteenth-century version of it, not a twenty-first-century one.

From the Constituent Assembly to the SC, this tussle has gone to extremes. The SC has ruled that practices 'essential' to a religion are constitutionally protected, and has even gone into assessing which controversial religious practices are essential.

Frankly, it is bizarre for constitutional judges to act as arbiters of religious authenticity. Where religious practices violate constitutional guarantees to individuals, secular States should unhesitatingly side with the latter—as, for example, the US SC did in overruling religious objections to vaccinations.

India faces similar tests. In one case being heard now, Justice D.Y. Chandrachud has said, 'SC judges are now assuming a theological mantle, which we are not expected to... The test should be whether a practice subscribes to the Constitution, irrespective of whether it is essential (to a religion) or not.'

Exactly.

This article was first published in *The Times of India* on 29 August 2018

5

ARRESTING DEVELOPMENTS

*In the Scheduled Caste and Scheduled Tribe (Prevention of
Atrocities) Act controversy, an irresistible force meets
an immovable object*

The SC's decision, that arrests made under the law on atrocities against SCs and tribals must meet a basic standard of due process, has unleashed protests, violence and deaths. This tension will not dissipate easily and deserves understanding, not to mention extremely careful handling.

Already sensitive about caste tensions impacting the electoral landscape, the Union government has filed a review petition. At issue are two opposing viewpoints that are like the proverbial meeting of an immovable object and an irresistible force.

On the one hand is the most fundamental tenet of law, that an accused person must be presumed to be innocent until proven guilty. This is the very basis of not just India's so-called 'adversarial' system of law (also followed in the UK and the US), but even alternate ones, like the inquisitorial system followed in countries like Sweden, France and Germany. In other words, this principle is intrinsic to modern, civilized and democratic societies.

On the other hand is the undeniable evidence that atavistic caste prejudices endure in twenty-first-century India. These range from everyday slights, social ostracism and discrimination at work, to intimidation and violence. This is despite seven decades of independence, a Constitution that grants every citizen equal status, and, indeed, laws to enforce those rights.

This failure to deliver justice results from bias and unequal power equations at the grass-roots level. Reports of SCs and tribals being intimidated or attacked for asserting their new-found freedoms, and of the police not registering first information reports (FIRs), are not exactly rare. Compounded by a broken prosecutorial system and huge backlogs in courts, it breeds impunity.

The response to that failure has been to legislate ever tougher measures against societal bias and discrimination. Caste is not the only area in which India has sought to compensate for the lack of enforcement of a law, by introducing summary penalties in that law. The same has happened with the law on domestic violence. In several such laws, now an accusation is not just sufficient to arrest someone, irrespective of prima facie evidence, but, in fact, also mandatory.

Political Correctness Overtakes Rational Discourse

The justification for this has been that India's deep-seated societal prejudices of caste and patriarchy often get in the way of the niceties of law. Therefore, to overcome bias in implementing such laws, summary steps, like arrests, must be made mandatory upon accusation alone.

While this approach addresses a genuine problem, it also creates new ones. In introducing mandatory punitive action without due process, it steps over the red line of the presumption of innocence.

That is precisely what the SC adjudicated: whether an accusation without prima facie evidence should be enough to deny anticipatory bail to the accused. While agreeing to hear the government's review petition, SC denied any interim relief, insisting that 'the law has not been diluted at all', by stipulating certain prerequisites to prevent arrests based on false accusations.

Here, political correctness overtakes rational discourse. Several commentators have claimed that there is no data on false accusations, but, in fact, the National Crime Records Bureau states that of 47,300 cases lodged in 2016 for atrocities against SCs/STs, 11 per cent (or 5,300) were found to be false. Fake accusations are the other side of the impunity coin, with little to no risk of punishment.

This is where the immovable object and the irresistible force collide. The age-old idea for legal systems to emphasize protecting the innocent over punishing the guilty goes back to Biblical times. This principle is exemplified by William Blackstone's famous dictum that a good legal system should rather let ten guilty people escape than convict one innocent. This principle was supported, to varying degrees, by other thinkers like Voltaire and Benjamin Franklin.

However, that principle is no succour to India's SCs and tribal citizens who have experienced discrimination, intimidation and violence. Others may not be able to evaluate that in the same gut-wrenching, soul-numbing and viscerally angry way.

A key argument by Attorney General K.K. Venugopal in the SC review petition is revealing. He argued that the burden of due process that the SC has now imposed for the Scheduled Caste and Scheduled Tribe (Prevention of Atrocities) [SC/ST PoA] law, to establish prima facie evidence or seek prior sanction before arrest, does not apply to identical circumstances of criminal law for the general population.

He is right, but what this implies is not that an accusation should be enough to arrest someone accused of any crime, but that India's criminal laws should be updated and similar standards of due process and probable cause be made applicable for most arrests. That is the norm in modern democracies.

What would really boost the enforcement of the SC/ST PoA Act is the provisioning of the much-needed infrastructure. To expedite cases and curb impunity, India needs special courts for it, in all 707 districts and not just the present 194. Equally, there must be strict penalties for perjury and false accusations, as recommended by a Parliamentary Standing Committee.

If we give up on the presumption of innocence, we would also be giving up on India as a democracy, where all citizens enjoy equal rights. However, that should not mean that we keep letting down our traditionally disenfranchised citizens. A basic shortcoming is the lack of resources, which we must determine to allocate.

This article was first published in *The Times of India* on 11 April 2018

6

A STEP FORWARD

To end child marriage, the Supreme Court must act decisively

India has the highest number of child brides in the world, according to a UN International Children's Emergency Fund (UNICEF) study conducted in 2016. As per the latest census, 30 per cent of married women in India wed before they turn eighteen. This is despite the fact that the Prohibition of Child Marriage Act (PCMA) 2006 set the legal age of marriage for women at eighteen years. The practice of underage marriage is also in direct violation of the UN Convention on Elimination of All Forms of Discrimination against Women, which India ratified back in 1993. In addition to deterring socio-economic empowerment of women by perpetuating the cycle of illiteracy and exploitation, child marriage is a severe impediment to maternal and child health. It is associated with a 50 per cent higher chance of stillbirth and death within the first few weeks among infants born to underage mothers.

While the number of child brides under fifteen has seen a decline, the rate of marriages has increased for girls between fifteen and eighteen, according to UNICEF. Therefore, for the law against child marriage to be truly effective, we must ensure that there are no other legal provisions that contravene it.

The SC as well as the Delhi HC are hearing separate cases with regard to the same provision—Exception 2 to Section 375 of the Indian Penal Code (IPC) on rape. Exception 2 states that 'sexual intercourse by a man with his wife, the wife not being under fifteen years of age, is not rape'. The existence of this section provides tacit approval to illegal marriages between the ages of fifteen and eighteen. Further, since the legal age of sexual consent under the

IPC is eighteen years, child marriage would amount to statutory rape, if not for the exception mentioned above.

The petition in the Delhi HC calls for the criminalization of marital rape. This is a larger issue that extends beyond underage brides. The SC, on the other hand, is looking into a narrower aspect of whether the law allows for sexual intercourse with minors in the case of married girls between the ages of fifteen and eighteen. While the Delhi HC hears different arguments, the SC has the opportunity to lay the groundwork for an in-principle recognition of marital rape as well as harmonize the legal provisions around the age of sexual consent under several existing laws that can fortify the law against child marriage.

First, the SC must determine if married women between fifteen and eighteen form a separate class from unmarried minors. The Protection of Children from Sexual Offences Act 2012, as well as the section on the age of consent as per the IPC, when read together, imply that sexual offences have been divided into two classes— sexual offences against minors, and sexual offences against women who have attained majority. In the first class, since it pertains to a minor, whether or not consent is given is deemed irrelevant as the minor is treated as incapable of giving any form of consent. In the second class, after a woman has attained the age of eighteen, she is deemed capable of giving consent, and thereafter, it must be considered in cases of sexual violence. If viewed from this restricted lens, coupled with the fact that PCMA sets eighteen years as the legal age of marriage, the provision to treat married women between fifteen and eighteen would appear invalid.

The Larger Picture

Unfortunately, this is not a one-dimensional issue, and the existence of personal laws has to be accommodated while looking at the larger picture. Muslim law, Christian law as well as the Hindu Marriage Act allow for minors to be married, with varying provisions for revocation of marriage. Various HCs have taken competing and contradictory views when it comes to whether the PCMA will prevail over personal laws. In 2014, the Gujarat HC held that a Muslim woman can get married by choice after reaching the age of fifteen and attaining puberty. On the other hand, several other jurisdictions—including the Delhi, Karnataka and Madras HCs—have taken the view that the PCMA must prevail over personal laws, including the Muslim personal law. But despite various HCs ruling in favour of the PCMA overriding personal laws, Karnataka is the only state to amend the PCMA and declare any marriage between minors as invalid by law. Clearly, there is a disparity and incoherence in terms of jurisprudence on this front. The current proceedings are an opportunity for the SC to minimize discretionary pronouncements with regard to the prevalence of personal laws, when it comes to child marriage.

With a view to making the provisions on underage marriage consistent with these laws, I have filed a private members' bill in the Parliament—the Criminal Law (Amendment) Bill 2017—that seeks to replace the word 'fifteen', mentioned in Exception 2, to 'eighteen'. A uniform age of consent and marriage will help solve several discrepancies between the legal age of marriage, the age of consent of an unmarried woman and Exception 2. It will provide protection for the physical and mental well-being of minor women, who are already victims of the societal evil of child marriage.

If anyone below eighteen is assumed to not have the capacity to form an informed decision when it comes to voting for a leader, I doubt they will have that faculty when it comes to marriage. Informed consent and the ability to form it, is the differentiating factor between the ages of fifteen and eighteen. The verdict of the SC is expected soon, and one hopes that the judiciary will take cognizance of this basic principle. The amendment to Section 375 will serve as a benchmark in creating more homogenous laws and will be a step forward in the abrogation of child marriage in India.

This article was first published in *The Asian Age* on 27 September 2017

7

A TURNING POINT FOR INDIA

The Supreme Court's triple talaq judgment sets the country on course to a uniform civil code

The landmark judgment by an SC Constitution Bench, outlawing instant 'triple talaq' divorce by Muslim men, is a turning point for the Indian republic and the very idea of India. This is despite the ruling being a hesitant, split verdict.

Admittedly, not everyone agrees with this assessment, and some even trivialize the parallels with the historic Shah Bano judgment of 1985. But make no mistake, this is a game changer. For starters, unlike the Shah Bano case that was overturned by an act of the Parliament in 1986, there is no chance of this being undone. In fact, it has already rekindled discussion on a uniform civil code (UCC), one of the unfulfilled 'directive principles' of India's Constitution that would replace the existing separate personal laws for Hindus, Muslims, Parsis and Christians. Those who opposed reforming the triple talaq had feared this, predicting that it would pave the way for a UCC. The irony, of course, is that many opponents had traditionally included not just conservative Muslims and religious leaders, but also 'secular' politicians and activists.

This interpretation of secularism—defending the rights of minority groups instead of individuals—was always at odds with the construct of a modern democracy whose Constitution guarantees equal rights to all citizens. However, it had its own rationale during the Mughal and colonial eras, and due to the turmoil that India underwent when it was partitioned and gained independence. That rationale is best understood by comparing the rights that minority groups have historically had in theocratic nations (both conservative and liberal) with the universal rights of all citizens in modern, secular democracies.

At one end of the spectrum are conservative theocracies like the Kingdom of Saudi Arabia, which disallows the public practice of religions other than its State version of Islam.

The middle of that spectrum is exemplified by the erstwhile Ottoman Empire: theocratic but relatively liberal. Though its conquest of Constantinople in 1453 was brutal—with massacres, plunder, enslavement and the conversion to Islam of many residents—by the sixteenth century, it had become much more tolerant. The Ottomans's 'Millet' system of jurisprudence allowed every religious community their own laws. This represented a kind of nationhood where the Muslim ruling class retained its pre-eminence but, in enlightened self-interest, also protected minorities by balancing their rights as a group.

At the other end of the nationhood yardstick are countries like the UK, the US, France and Germany. Evolving from monarchies to liberal democracies, they dispensed with both privileges for the majority community, as well as group rights for minorities, replacing them with common rights for all individual citizens.

In the tumult leading up to India's independence, the idea that we could aspire to be a modern democratic republic was not accepted widely enough; thus, the two-nation theory—the idea of Pakistan, and partition.

Nevertheless, our republic's founders were committed to a modern, secular democracy, not a theocratic Hindu mirror image of Pakistan. However, in their anxiety to reassure the remaining minorities, they did not immediately push through the modern, democratic version of secularism.

Instead, though they spelled out that aim in the directive principles, in the interim, they decided to continue with the existing Raj-era separate personal laws. Limited progress thereafter includes the enactment of laws against dowry and domestic violence, Hindu personal laws and the optional Special

Marriage Act, all reflecting modern sensibilities.

However, despite becoming an established and respected democracy, our medieval kind of secularism had remained like that of the Ottoman Empire's (balancing group rights), rather than like modern, democratic republics (focusing on individual rights).

The Idea of India

While the above might have been expedient to hold together a splintered nation during its initial birth pangs as a republic, the underlying premise is deeply troubling in the long run, for it reinforces the two-nation theory. Separate laws for every religious group in a modern democracy can be justified only if we accept that the majority cannot be trusted to uphold the individual rights of minorities.

In fact, that is precisely what critics of UCC argue, whether explicitly or couched in euphemisms. They cite various aberrations over the past seventy years, including the recent cow vigilantism, to assert that India is 'not ready' for a UCC.

However, in reality, despite its many problems, India has proved to be a stable democracy where such horrors are the exception, not the norm. Moreover, institutions like the judiciary and the EC continue to inspire confidence, as in the SC's other landmark judgment that made privacy a fundamental right.

Cynicism about the UCC undermines the idea of India as prescribed by the Constitution. Moreover, it does disservice to both our hard-won democracy as well as to those who would allegedly suffer when a UCC is implemented.

The largely positive reactions to the 'triple talaq' judgment show that India has come a long way in the past three decades. The court should, perhaps, have determined the triple talaq's constitutional validity without going into its religious standing. Be that as it may, ruling that a codified religious personal law is unconstitutional opens the door to full-fledged secularism.

Those who worry that India might become a 'Hindu Pakistan'

should take note of a new Pakistani law enacted earlier this year, the Hindu Marriage Act. If we are not to be a mirror image of that theocratic nation, this is a reflection we should not want.

This article was first published in *The Times of India* on 30 August 2017

8

A FUNDAMENTAL RIGHT

After the 'right to privacy' ruling, focus must now be on creating robust data protection laws

Technological advancements directly affect the contours of privacy in the twenty-first century. Presently, India has an Internet penetration of about 31 per cent and in the coming years, it has the potential to boom, much like—or perhaps faster than—the cell phone phenomenon. The size of an individual's digital footprint is dramatically expanding every day, with a plethora of information readily available to them. Experts have gone to the extent of saying that there is technology that can analyse individuals by simply reviewing a few hundred 'likes' on Facebook and 'know you better than your spouse'. Similarly, Aadhaar, which forms an essential part of the government's flagship JAM trinity—Jan Dhan, Aadhaar, mobile—for better governance, is being couched as an insurmountable 'big brother' threat to privacy. The discourse around this is starkly divided between those who consider privacy intrusions to be inevitable and those who are advocating privacy as an absolute right. Such a binary approach is unlikely to amount to any pragmatic solution.

Exceptions to the Right to Privacy

The right to privacy, while fundamental, must make room for some accurately and narrowly defined exceptions. The SC has expounded a three-tier test for any exception to be made to the right to privacy—legality (which postulates the existence of the law), legitimate State aim, i.e. the need for invasion and proportionality (which ensures a rational connection between the ends), and the means adopted to achieve them. According to the verdict, legitimate aims of the State, for which the invasion of privacy can be permitted, includes 'preventing the dissipation of social welfare benefits'. This outlook permits the continuation of Aadhaar for the purposes of distribution of welfare benefits, and prevents any further 'dissipation'. Thus, the Aadhaar initiative can not only coexist with the status of privacy as a fundamental right, but can also flourish as a viable system of welfare distribution and lead to increased financial inclusion.

Going forward, the interpretation of 'legitimate State aim' must be narrowly tailored, as observed by Justice Jasti Chelameswar. A good reference point for this may be found in the higher standard of limitations to speech laws in the US as compared to India.

In the context of free speech, the Brandenburg test is the gold standard, which lays emphasis on 'imminent lawless action' and the 'likelihood to incite such action' being directly related to any form of speech for it to warrant action restraining it. In India, well-intentioned 'reasonable restrictions' have, thus far, been vague and broad, making them prone to misuse. We must evolve legislation around privacy in a manner that our emphasis is on narrowly defined exceptions to prevent arbitrary abuse.

Data Protection

The right to privacy encompasses the right to have our data protected. This rights-based approach allows citizens complete control over their data—consent for any kind of usage, processing, sharing with third parties (or even removal), and the 'right to be forgotten'.

Every day, we face the threat of data breaches and financial frauds leading to monetary losses. In 2017, reports of malware and ransomware have become commonplace. In 2016, a sum of ₹1.3 crore was reportedly lost in fraudulent transactions because of a malware attack on debit card details. In fact, our financial data is so vulnerable that out of all kinds of data breaches in 2016, 73 per cent were based on unauthorized access to financial data and identity thefts.

These facts may seem alarming at first, but it is important to take a step back and look at the huge and proven benefits of big data as well. For example, let's look at health innovations that are being guided and shaped by big data globally. Technological giants like Google and Amazon are using their big data capabilities in furthering groundbreaking medical research related to critical health challenges like cancer. Grass-root governance is witnessing a paradigm shift from the age-old tradition of corruption and leakages in the targeted delivery to those in need.

Should we act as gatekeepers and resist innovation being brought in by a global technological revolution? A cynic may go to the extent of saying that if our data is being mined, perhaps we should just sell it for a nominal price. This may hold some appeal or a morsel of reason, but it would be a short-sighted approach. Instead of giving up autonomy over our data, shouldn't our efforts be directed towards safeguarding our data?

The Need for a Data Protection Law

In the age of machine learning algorithms, our focus should be on tighter regulation of data and making data handlers, both government and private, accountable. Recent US government research showed that while determining the creditworthiness of someone utilizing the facility of digital loans, there was a bias hurting the scores of younger borrowers, as people with lower incomes were targeted for higher interest rates. To import this to the Indian scenario, there is a possibility that similar machine learning algorithms could display a bias towards farmers or members of a particular community, based on the criteria of low income. Therefore, as recommended by a study by the Ford Foundation, which discusses this issue at length, we must invest in developing a greater cohort of public interest technologists who can review and correct such flaws in algorithms. With the growing emphasis on 'Digital India' and financial inclusion, it is likely that situations like these will manifest with greater frequency in the future. This calls for a regulatory authority with power, inter alia, to conduct inspections or algorithm audits of entities, both government and private, which deal with data.

There is a dire requirement for India to address the concerns around data security by mandating prompt response to data breaches and the fortification of security by government or private entities. Compliance has to be ensured through adequate punitive measures and hefty fines. Transparency arising out of the shift of the implementation and compliance burden on to the actual handlers of our data will promote greater trust in the data ecosystem.

The right to privacy has been declared a fundamental right, but to prevent financial losses or any other kind of misuse of data, further steps need to be taken. The nine-judge bench of the SC has traced the evolution of an individual's right to privacy, but the way forward has to be charted through a robust data protection law.

This article was first published in *The Wire* on 25 August 2017

9

AADHAAR AND DATA SECURITY

Irrespective of what one feels about Aadhaar,
a comprehensive new privacy law is needed

Aadhaar, India's biometric identification system, which is the largest such project in the world, is in the eye of a storm after being made mandatory for tax returns. The SC has started hearing a PIL challenging this, and both social and traditional media are abuzz with strong views on the topic.

In 2017, I filed in the Parliament, a private members' bill on data privacy and protection, and even much before that, have been advocating the overhaul of our woefully obsolete and fragmented laws with a comprehensive new Act. However, this is far from being a black-and-white issue, and there are many nuances that deserve more deliberation.

Though Aadhaar has become the focal point of this debate, threats to data security and citizens' rights to privacy go far beyond it. In fact, as its creator and the Information Technology industry's wunderkind Nandan Nilekani puts it: if a malicious hacker or secretive agency were to try hacking one's privacy, cracking Aadhaar would figure low on their list of ways to go about it.

There is already vast information about us, including biometrics, out there in the cloud, with more being collected every day. This happens through malware, covert eavesdropping and the mindless permissions we voluntarily grant SM sites and apps. There is now a growing global movement to treat data as one of the world's most valuable resources and, just like oil was a century ago, to tightly regulate it in public interest.

Just as antitrust laws were passed in the US more than a century ago, to break up the dominant Standard Oil Company, now even that flag-bearer of free markets, *The Economist*, has endorsed a call to break open the data dominance of internet giants like Google, Amazon, Apple, Facebook and Microsoft. However, even ardent trustbusters recognize the immense benefits to humankind from technologies that such companies have developed, and expressly seek to preserve these, aiming only to prevent the abuse of dominant power.

Understanding the True Potential

By contrast, many pro-privacy and data protection activists in India are largely in denial about the benefits of Aadhaar, while correctly seeking to plug the threats related to it. Ironically, when it comes to other risky aspects of our growing connectedness, such as online financial transactions, even the most passionate activists seek reasonable security measures, not outright bans or curtailment.

Our approach to Aadhaar must be the same: taking advantage of its immense potential for good, while putting in place a modern legal framework to prevent abuse. Aadhaar has already led to the plugging of significant 'leakages'—a polite term for massive corruption—but the potential is far, far more.

Many people remember late PM Rajiv Gandhi's comment, in the '80s, that only fifteen paise of every rupee spent by the government ever reached beneficiaries. Newer data from the erstwhile Planning Commission between 2005 and 2014 revealed that 40–73 per cent of the money spent on the PDS never reached beneficiaries.

Similarly, mind-boggling amounts of tax are evaded in India by the simple tactic of maintaining multiple PAN cards, which are required for bank accounts and big transactions. India has approximately 19 million IT-payers versus 250 million PAN cards, and there is no way to deduplicate the latter without Aadhaar. There are several such examples of large-scale fraud or inefficiencies that could also be cleaned up.

The conflation of the alleged leakage of Aadhaar numbers, like the leakage of the underlying biometrics, may be confusing to some.

Nevertheless, whether cavalier or criminal, such misuse of private data is unconscionable and should be subject to punishment. In any event, irrespective of what one feels about Aadhaar, a comprehensive new data protection and privacy law is needed to supersede the inadequate and overlapping Indian Telegraph Act (1885), as well as the Information Technology Act (2000) and its rules (2011).

The data protection aspect of such a law must emphasize a person's rights to his/her personal data; require his/her informed consent to collect, process, remove or alter such data; oblige those who deal with data to keep it secure; and have a grievance mechanism to punish violations with hefty fines and imprisonment.

However, the privacy aspect of any new law is bound to be complex, and will, undoubtedly, stir even more controversy. Indian laws don't provide for a specific right to privacy, though court judgments have defined certain limited rights, and the SC has admitted yet another PIL on the topic.

Meanwhile, some activists' insistence on citizens' absolute right to privacy will inevitably run afoul of security considerations, including, in some cases, national security. In this age of terrorism, the issue of surveillance will be a major point of debate. Standards will be needed, which permit the anonymous surveillance of metadata, such as algorithms that flag frequent references to, say, 'RDX' in emails, with prima facie evidence and warrants being required for further snooping.

Like it or not, we have already ceded rights to absolute privacy, such as with body scanners by airport security, and the widespread adoption of closed-circuit television cameras. New technologies enable these to have biometric capabilities too, allowing individual identification similar to Aadhaar.

This should not mean that more concessions of privacy are to be wantonly permitted, but neither should it mean the imposition of unreasonable, impractical rules that thwart twenty-first-century life.

This article was first published in *The Times of India* on 10 May 2017

10

NET NEUTRAL, SHIFT GEARS

*Now we must push for forceful measures to extend full
Internet access to all Indians*

India's battle for net neutrality was won, with the Telecom
Regulatory Authority of India's 2016 ruling going against
Facebook's so-called 'Free Basics' service. However, for those of us
who had spoken in favour of net neutrality, it is not a time for
celebrations. Rather, it is time to speak equally forcefully for steps
to extend full Internet access to the vast majority of Indians still
without it.

It would be unconscionable not to do so; for, despite its many
shortcomings, Free Basics did have one argument in its favour, that
some connectivity is better than none. Nevertheless, history shows
that the full, unfragmented Internet is assuredly far, far superior. It
was worth fighting for it to prevail, but the victory would be pyrrhic,
unless Internet access becomes ubiquitous.

It is said that those who do not learn from history are doomed
to repeat it. Many people arguing on this topic seemed blissfully
unaware of the Internet's history, which is relevant for India's policy
choices today. But first, a disclosure: I have family business interests
that could have benefited from the lack of net neutrality.

Many do know, of course, that the Internet was originally a US
government defence project that was later opened up for use by the
public. It was not the only one, with another being the satellite-
based global positioning system for navigation. This was apparently
forgotten by laissez-faire supporters of Free Basics, who abhorred
any governmental 'interference' in how the digital divide should
be bridged.

In fact, although the Internet was opened to the public much earlier, it was not until a historic 1996 US legislation guaranteeing equal access, that it could overcome the iron grip of fragmented but entrenched, oligopolistic communications networks. From the '70s through the mid-90s, companies like CompuServe and America Online dominated the pre-Internet data communications space.

They were cutting edge for the time, and subscribers could message, participate on discussion boards, post classifieds, and so on. However, they were 'walled gardens' (that is, closed user groups not connected to each other) and did not unleash the enormous benefits that the wide-open Internet would. More importantly, their corporate owners wielded enormous power over what users could leverage those networks for, which resulted in stifling competition and innovation.

It was not until President Bill Clinton pushed through the Telecommunications Act of 1996, that a major breakthrough occurred. Replacing an obsolete 1934 Act, it levelled the playing field for all forms of telecommunications. This stimulated competition among entrenched telecom giants and also gave a huge boost to new Internet service providers. The rest is history. Closed user groups fell by the wayside and the open Internet grew exponentially. This made possible previously unimaginable services and innovations, including the success of Facebook itself and many others like it.

It was, thus, ironic for Facebook to try and leverage its size to recreate walled gardens all over again, in the biggest market where the Internet is still beyond the reach of most. In any event, it has now withdrawn Free Basics from India, though not without churlish comments by one of its board members. There really is no free lunch, and letting giant companies re-establish oligopolistic, closed-group networks is not the answer.

As long ago as the '90s, the late, visionary head of the National Association of Software and Services Companies, Dewang Mehta, had proposed that all Indians must be assured of the modern basics, which he called 'roti, kapda, makaan, bijli aur bandwidth' (food, clothing, housing, electricity and bandwidth)—not bandwidth to only a few closed user groups controlled by a giant corporation with its own objectives, but plain vanilla, open, unfragmented and high-speed Internet bandwidth.

Connecting Millions

So, how do we go about connecting the hundreds of millions who are still without Internet access? The answer is simple: by using funds that the government has explicitly collected for this very objective, and by policy changes in line with global norms.

Many countries cross-subsidize within key sectors that ought to reach all citizens, like aviation and telecom. They impose a regulatory fee on operators in lucrative markets and then use that money to extend services to less attractive markets. India does this too, but has misused it. The Comptroller and Auditor General of India reported that of the nearly ₹59,000 crore raised from 2002–14 for the telecom Universal Service Obligation Fund (USOF), nearly ₹33,000 crore was diverted to uses other than funding rural telecom and the Internet!

This is now being corrected, with ₹72,000 crore of the USOF funding earmarked for the National Optical Fibre Network, to extend broadband to every panchayat. This was sorely needed, since our twenty-year obsession with spectrum had meant the total neglect of all other technologies, some of which have bigger global footprints.

But, more is needed, including making the USOF funds available to the private sector to foster competition, particularly as viability gap for last-mile rural connectivity, through reverse auctions.

Finally, competition-stifling policy bottlenecks must go. One glaring example is India's unusual restrictions on connecting Internet voice telephony to mobile and landline networks. This has enabled telecom companies to continue enjoying traditional voice service revenues, while staving off Internet voice competition.

Allow these, like most nations do, and see how telecom companies and others scramble to push Internet connectivity.

This article was first published in *The Times of India* on 17 February 2016

11

INDIA'S GREEK TRAGEDY

Re-examining the contentious issue of land acquisition

India is not the only country with a widespread belief in 'exceptionalism'. Wikipedia describes the term as 'the perception that a country, society, movement, or time period is unusual or extraordinary in some way, and thus, does not need to conform to normal rules or general principles'.

Many nations, both big and small, have also had histories of believing that they are qualitatively different from other countries. Nevertheless, human societies have obvious underlying commonalities, and it can often be helpful to juxtapose the challenges we face with the experience of others.

It is worth examining the contentious issue of land acquisition in this context. While in India, the raging debate on land acquisition centres on land owners' consent, it is revealing that neither in the US nor in China—which are at opposite ends of systems of governance—is any consent required when land is acquired for public purpose. It is a crucial contrast, for it goes to the heart of questions like:

- Whether our policymakers are looking for pragmatic solutions, or they are content to screech at each other.
- Whether we are ready to finally accept that though much can be done to improve farming, it is simply unsustainable for the sector to continue to provide livelihoods to 60 per cent of our population.
- Whether our farmers' children can have realistic alternate career opportunities or are destined to be

trapped in evermore fragmented, marginal farming.

- And finally, whether we, as a nation, at all believe that it is possible to create millions of jobs in manufacturing and services.

During the years-long process that led to the Land Acquisition, Rehabilitation and Resettlement (LARR) Act of 2013, the two most controversial aspects of the national debate were the consent of land losers and the compensation that they, and those employed on their land, ought to get. Till then, a nineteenth-century Raj-era law had often been abused to dispossess farmers and others at a fraction of what would become the market price of their land, after usage restrictions were lifted.

The issue of what percentage of the landowners concerned would need to consent to an acquisition went through many convoluted iterations. An empowered group of ministers' subcommittee of the Cabinet turned out to be not-so-empowered after all, when its recommendation was overruled and increased to 70 per cent (and 80 per cent for private companies). In scheduled areas, this was further compounded by other overlapping laws, which essentially gave a veto to each panchayat, rather than, say, a majority of them in the entire area being acquired.

Lessons from Around the World

Even at that time, the above were widely considered unworkable. The experience of these intervening months has only made that clearer, as even most of those opposing the recent changes admit in private. Of course, we don't need to blindly emulate other countries and must discern between their practices—and, to some degree, we have.

For instance, the Chinese definition of 'public purpose' is vague, whereas India's is specific. However, our definition is far narrower than in the US, where, in some cases, private development has been deemed to constitute public purpose. Similarly, the US emphasis on 'just compensation' for acquired land is worthy of emulation and our 2013 LARR Act goes to great lengths to ensure fair compensation and rehabilitation. Oddly, the initial outrage at the proposed new legislation included allegations that the compensation clauses were being rolled back. Whether that was deliberate or not, it quickly became apparent that that was not true, and the debate has since remained focused on consent and other procedural aspects.

Once again, the studies, procedures and clearances mandated by the 2013 Act go far beyond what either the US or China follow, requiring a minimum of fifty months for projects to get the go-ahead. This assumes that every stage of a complicated series of steps would work like clockwork, without any delays or extensions. Anyone who understands anything about the viability of infrastructure projects would know that this is a sure-fire way to make them unviable. Such provisions may be ideal from the perspective of a certain kind of philosophy—against industrialization and the post-industrial economy per se—but can hardly be expected to cater to the million-plus jobs that India now needs to create every month. As some countries have learnt at great cost (for instance, Greece, on the issue of fiscal discipline), we can defy global logic only at our own peril.

To those genuinely seeking solutions, it is equally critical to recognize that scepticism about fair compensation, and whether lost land can translate to jobs, is rooted in experience. For instance, there are still disputed compensation and employment claims from the '50s, when the government acquired land for major dams, steel plants and the like.

Instead of looking in the rear-view mirror at what has not worked in the past, we would be better served to benchmark what works in most of the world. It is incumbent on the government now to ensure that compensation is unclogged and front-ended, infrastructure is expedited, new jobs are made visible and education is reformed to promote employability. If we don't—counterintuitive as this may sound—some of the worst-affected will be India's farmers.

This article was first published in *The Times of India* on 18 March 2015

12

THE BITE IS BACK ONLINE

You cannot have free speech without
occasionally giving offence to someone

When the SC struck down Section 66A of the Information Technology Act in 2015, it upheld a long tradition of rulings mostly in favour of free speech. This judgment, in a PIL filed by law student Shreya Singhal, held the clause against posting 'grossly offensive' content online unconstitutional. The problem always was that the description was too vague: what is offensive to me may not be offensive to someone else. Who was to be the arbiter of what offends?

However, there were deeper issues at stake: should giving offence be a crime at all? Why should punishment for online offence be harsher than that for the same offence offline? What is the extent to which the Constitution guarantees free speech? With school and college students, cartoonists and professors being arrested for online posts, something had to give.

I enthusiastically welcomed the court's decision. When Singhal's PIL was filed in 2012, I was quoted as hoping it would succeed. That was the occasion of my filing a private members' bill in the Lok Sabha, seeking drastic dilution of Section 66A. My only regret is that, once again, it had to be the judiciary rather than the Parliament that set right an insidious law.

Evolution of the Law

Laws about the freedom of expression have evolved, not just in India but also in other democracies, over long periods of time.

Historically, the big breakthrough for free speech came in Europe, from the fourteenth through the eighteenth centuries. The Renaissance, the Reformation and the Age of Enlightenment saw science and reason break the grip of religion and the Church. Most importantly, these changes saw the decriminalization of blasphemy—which, till then, had been a heinous crime, attracting capital punishment, as it still does in some theocratic States.

This was crucial, for if giving offence to someone regarding something as sensitive as religion was no longer a crime, freedom of speech about almost everything else became far stronger. That is not to say that free speech is absolute, whether in Europe or elsewhere, but more on that shortly. In India, the debate on free speech—at least among common citizens, if not academics—is often stuck at the stage of 'people should have a right to say what they want, but not to offend someone else'.

From the eighteenth century onwards, it is the US that has been held up as the exemplar of free speech, what with its celebrated First Amendment. Indeed, the right to freedom of expression in that country is as close as it gets to absolute: you can't be arrested for even such inflammatory acts as burning the national flag or a holy book. However, all nations have restraints, such as those against deliberate and malicious defamation. The US has the narrowest-defined exceptions to freedom of expression—child pornography, for instance. However, even in the case of hate speech or incitement to violence, it requires 'clear and present danger' and 'imminent threat' to public order, before the authorities can intervene.

What is often not clearly understood, even among champions of US-style free speech, is that those rights evolved over two centuries. They were clarified and enhanced by many significant judgments. The SC ruling on Section 66A refers to many of these judgments from the US and the UK, besides domestic precedents. Our Constitution guarantees the freedom of speech, subject to 'reasonable restrictions', including 'security of the State, friendly relations with foreign States, public order, morality and defamation'.

The decades since 1947 have seen, sadly, efforts by the Parliament and assemblies to legislate the curbing of free expression even further. The authorities, too, are enthusiastic about implementing such laws. A recent egregious example from India saw a British Raj law being used to arrest a cartoonist for sedition. The UK had itself repealed its sedition law in 2009. Luckily for India, its highest court, like those of other liberal democracies, has consistently worked to uphold free speech. Often (though not always), HCs have followed the example of the SC. Acquitting cartoonist Aseem Trivedi, the Bombay HC judges noted that they didn't find the cartoons funny, but ruled that citizens are entitled to criticize a government: criticism cannot be considered sedition as long as it 'does not incite violence against the government or has the intention of creating public disorder'. I had filed another private members' bill in the Lok Sabha on similar lines; thankfully, it might no longer be required.

As India's judiciary keeps narrowing down exceptions to the freedoms guaranteed by our Constitution, it will become evermore important for our citizens to support this evolution. We need to recognize that one cannot have free speech without occasionally giving offence to another, and that being obnoxious should be distinguished from causing actual harm.

This article was first published in *Outlook* on 6 April 2015

SIX

◆

CITIZENS AND SOCIETY: HOLDING UP A MIRROR TO TWENTY-FIRST-CENTURY INDIA

While we are nearing the end of the second decade of the twenty-first century, many debates from earlier decades, centuries and even millennia continue unabated—and unresolved. Take religious freedoms for example—they are something that ancient India debated, fought over, and ultimately guaranteed, not just to its own denizens but for countless others fleeing persecution from their lands. The modern republic's Constitution guarantees it too, but there are many aspects and nuances of it that are still being fought over.

The story is similar on women's rights and other topics concerning empowerment of disadvantaged sections. India, like other democratic societies, has seen its share of activism aimed at correcting atavistic biases and injustices. As in those societies, much of that activism has centered on affirmative action of one kind or another.

As in other sections, the chapters in this section examine these issues with candour, and a commitment to the kind of reforms needed for a fairer society. Yet, avoiding the slippery slopes of moral flexibility and avoiding the seemingly easy path of political correctness with no concern for the basics of fairness and equal rights for all has also been a key objective of these articles.

Equally at play, are contrasting approaches to finding solutions for the problems that are still plaguing us. On the one hand are the frustrations of large sections of the public fed up with systemic failures and baying for blunt, populist solutions. Dismissing them by taking a moral high ground is theoretically easy, but the morality of such a path is compromised by the lack of actual solutions.

Finding the balance between an adherence to basic democratic principles and the pressing compulsions for simple, blunt solutions is one of the greatest challenges of modern democracies. This is especially so in the present era, when economically successful authoritarian societies like China are challenging the status quo, and even provoking a debate about the virtues of more decisive political systems.

India is the biggest democracy that has ever existed, with each successive general election setting new records of voting by the largest number of people. It is also unique in being a 'Big Bang' democracy—as the largest country ever to eschew the traditional path of evolving democratic systems over centuries.

No one has doubted whether India's democracy is real or robust, for many decades now. That used to be commonplace in the first few decades of the republic, but the questions thereafter have shifted—to whether the inherently slower decision-making that this entails is imposing too high a cost, especially compared to other nations that have scaled up the ladder of economic progress much faster, while leaving the development of democracy for later.

But recent years have started demonstrating that the trajectory is shifting upwards and that the future may benefit from a 'tipping point' effect, rather than being bound to a simple, linear extrapolation of the past. The India of today is aspirational in a way that could not have been believed till merely a generation ago.

Decades of diffidence have given way to an emerging confidence. This is all to the good. Yet, there are legacy issues that cannot just be ignored or hoped to be resolved by themselves. You can see all this as a glass half full or half empty. I remain an optimist, but one that believes that rather than just *hoping* for the best, we have to keep attempting to *solve* lingering problems.

1

LOSING MY RELIGION

If minority communities have the right to convert others,
then so does the majority

During the framing of India's Constitution, the matter of whether it should guarantee the right to not just freely profess and practise one's religion but also to propagate it, was much debated. Ultimately, Article 25 of the Constitution guarantees all three, but subject to 'public order, morality and health'.

The Hindu right has often accused Christian and Muslim proselytizers of using inducement or coercion to get Hindus to convert. Missionaries from those religions—as well as secular, liberal activists—have invariably opposed such accusations and have stood in favour of ensuring constitutional protection for propagating religion. Ironically, neither side has been consistent in the principles of its stand, sometimes arguing in opposite directions depending on who the converters are, and who, the converted.

Though Hinduism is not considered a proselytizing religion, Hindu missionaries is not exactly a new phenomenon. The ancient evangelist Adi Shankaracharya led a movement to revitalize Hinduism, in light of the growth of Buddhism, and the first modern-day Hindu missionary effort, seeking to reconvert those whose ancestors had left the fold, was the Arya Samaj Shuddhi movement of the early twentieth century. It faced fierce resistance, culminating in the assassination of Swami Shraddhanand in 1926.

Born that year, was the man who later became known as Swami Lakshmanananda Saraswati, another Hindu missionary, who was also killed in 2008, triggering the riots in Odisha's Kandhamal district. However, violence has not been the preserve of any one group, as the murder, also in Odisha, of Australian Christian missionary Graham Staines and his two minor sons proved in 1999.

Old and New Fault Lines

Recent incidents of conversion have reignited the issue, with sections of the Opposition resolutely stopping the Parliament from functioning, particularly the Rajya Sabha, where the government is in a minority. In the process, however, both old and new fault lines are on display.

Many in the Opposition, who have, in the past, stoutly defended the right of the minorities to proselytize—and rejected allegations of coercion or inducement—are today taking the exactly opposite stand when it concerns proselytizing by the majority. Moreover, just as blatantly, some of those who have energetically opposed minority missionaries are adopting both their tactics and their arguments.

Though today, it is a BJP government and its supporters who are suggesting a national law to regulate conversions, such suggestions have come in the past too, when the Congress was in government. Bills were proposed to be introduced in the Parliament in 1954, 1960 and 1979, but fell through for lack of support. However, upon mass conversions in Meenakshipuram in 1981, it was a Congress-led Union government that advised all states to enact laws regulating conversions.

Such laws have been passed by several states and have even withstood constitutional challenges. The first two were by Odisha (as far back as 1967) and then Madhya Pradesh (1968). Both wound their way to the SC, where a constitution bench upheld them. The SC's ruling was based on the public order caveat of the constitutional guarantee, as well as its determination that both the states' laws guaranteed religious freedom to all. The SC's ruling also held that while Article 25 of the Constitution grants the freedom of conscience to all—as also the right to transmit or spread one's religion by an exposition of its tenets—it does not confer the right to convert another person to one's own religion.

Subsequently, Chhattisgarh (2000), Gujarat (2003), Himachal Pradesh (2006) and Rajasthan (2008) have passed laws to regulate conversions. Tamil Nadu had passed its anti-forcible conversion law in 2002, but repealed it in 2005. Incidentally, state laws regulating conversions are not just a post-independence feature. In British India, the princely states of Raigarh, Patna and Udaipur had far more rigid laws, which, in fact, were aimed squarely at preventing conversions to Christianity.

Nevertheless, the UN rapporteur for religious freedom, Heiner Bielefeldt, has said that these state laws undermine religious freedom in India. Despite lauding India as the birthplace of many religions and its heritage of pluralism, he asserts that the requirement of converts having to explain their reasons for conversion is humiliating and wrongly attributes the state with somehow having the ability to assess its genuineness.

Though the UN rapporteur concedes that coercion must be prevented, he also states that such concepts as inducement or allurement are not only vague, but that 'any invitation to another religion has elements of inducement or allurement'. He notes that these are 'loosely defined terms' and don't meet the standards of criminal justice, in which 'laws need to be clear'.

So, would a national law help? Could it be precise and clear, thus giving force to the Constitution's provisions—both its rights and protections? Might it help overcome the current contradictions? After all, since all sides have indulged in propagating their religions—and faced accusations of coercing, inducing and alluring—it is theoretically possible to agree on a minimum definition of acceptable norms that are compatible with the Constitution.

But in practice, it is highly unlikely that there can be any such consensus across the political spectrum on a new law regulating conversions, clear or otherwise. If the issue lingers on, sooner or later the nation's highest court will have to step in again.

This article was first published in *The Times of India* on 25 December 2014

2

PERCEPTIONS MATTER

It's no coincidence that the narrative of rising intolerance has been peaking around the elections

It has been a while now, since news reports of attacks on churches in India disappeared from the headlines—and thank goodness for that! Yet, for a while, a few years ago, such reports had seemed to dominate the news, at least in the mainstream English media if not in its much larger vernacular cousins, nationwide. In hindsight, it can be useful to examine what happened, as well as assess other allegations and reports of intolerance that have now taken centre stage.

Did the reports of church attacks fade away because, as Vatican Radio reported, after many months, 'prominent Christian leaders (felt the government was finally showing) genuine concern over attacks on the minority community', causing a sudden cessation of violence? Or was it the case, as argued by many equally prominent voices, that a handful of isolated incidents, some of which were clearly not of a communal nature, had been played up into something worse?

The latter argument is bolstered by the fact that even larger numbers of robberies, vandalism and desecration of other places of worship rarely get reported in the media—for instance, on Christmas eve in 2014, there was a rather spectacular robbery and desecration of a famous temple in my constituency. Despite creating much consternation locally, the incident barely registered in the regional media, and didn't get even a passing mention, nationally. Fortunately, it was not communal in nature and, equally importantly, no one tried to claim it was.

However, discontinued stories of church attacks have given way to a sustained and broader narrative of intolerance against minorities—again, much more so in the English rather than vernacular media. Then, as now, the allegations are that fringe elements with political connections to the government have become emboldened and are fanning confrontations from the controversies over beef and ink attacks, all the way up to a mob lynching.

This narrative continues to be countered by arguments from the right, which essentially claims that there is no increase in the frequency of such incidents, and that a long-entrenched left liberal ecosystem is resisting its political marginalization by deliberately, selectively and hypocritically playing them up.

This stand has got some support, albeit qualified, from even respectable bastions of liberalism. The BBC, for example, commented in 2015 that 'there certainly wasn't a shortage of religious intolerance before Modi was elected'. Even prominent author Taslima Nasreen, while supporting protesting writers, had commented on the biases of some Indian liberals.

A Narrative of Rising Intolerance

Articulate, prominent voices on both sides continue to duke it out, debating whether the statistics indicate a rising trend of intolerance, and if the statistics matter or whether the perception is already bad enough. They are also dissecting instances of reverse intolerance for, and against, the charge of selective outrage. Relying on statistics can be a slippery slope, at least in the short term. The BBC blog referred to an Indian newspaper report indicating a year-on-year 25 per cent rise in communal incidents in the first five months of 2015. Yet, the same newspaper had earlier reported, on the topic of church attacks, that the numbers were no different than in the previous two years.

As the journalist and author Anand Ranganathan pointed out, some of the commentators who cite statistics to claim rising intolerance, often fail to acknowledge previous years' data— for example, on average, two communal incidents per day in 2011–13.

In any event, it is surely no coincidence that—real or exaggerated—this narrative of rising intolerance has been peaking around elections. Just as in the earlier phase of reported church attacks bunched around the Delhi state election, similarly, now the crucial Bihar election is undoubtedly a catalyst. The bigger question is: for whom? For, no one side or party has a monopoly on such tactics.

Because this government is, above all, a Narendra Modi government, a big part of the narrative focuses on whether the PM is doing enough to tackle the situation. Although he has spoken against communalism on several occasions, inside and outside the Parliament, the debate still rages as to whether he has spoken out enough, whether he has spoken swiftly enough and whether he has done enough.

Some commentators and public intellectuals, who are supportive of the PM, have questioned the idea that he ought to speak out more, concluding that if he were to react to every alleged or real communal incident, he would have time for little else. They are convinced that his opponents have succeeded in setting him up and that he must devote himself to real issues of governance rather than perceptions of rising intolerance.

Nevertheless, even some of his staunchest supporters are now joining the chorus that he ought to say and do more. At the very least, they recognize the power of perception for earning or dissipating political capital.

In fact, many insiders are even acknowledging the damage caused by the irresponsible statements and actions of some of their fellow travellers. This has been apparently addressed by what is said to be an internal ticking off, behind closed doors. However, only time will tell whether it was real or just a rap on the knuckles, and whether it will actually lead to contrition.

This article was first published in *The Times of India* on 28 October 2015

3

SABARIMALA AND TRIPLE TALAQ

*The two situations are different; the courts
should not judge them the same way*

Many people are keen that temples like Sabarimala should remove restrictions on female devotees, but also that these come about through religious reform from within the community, rather than a court verdict. Some may believe that the recent SC ruling that enforces reform promotes secularism; in fact, it does the opposite.

So, should the State—government, legislature or court—never intervene in religious practices? What about the banning of sati, caste discrimination and, as happened recently, instant triple talaq? There, I believe, the State was justified in intervening.

What is the distinction, you ask? Plenty.

Before addressing the differences in those situations, it is important to understand that the prevailing Indian iteration of secularism is different from what the term usually means in modern democracies—which is the separation of Church and State. As should only be expected, India's attempt to 'treat all religions equally' is plagued by subjectivity that undermines secularism.

This subjectivity has led to a bizarre situation, where the majority religion in India experiences extraordinary interference from the State, unlike anything seen elsewhere. It is almost as if the Indian State distrusts Hindus and, throwing aside all pretence of secularism, exercises direct control over their religious institutions.

In India, Hindu places of worship—and Hinduism *alone*—experience the following: control and management by the government, including altering religious rituals; government control over administrative and financial decisions, including diverting income for other purposes; temple income being subject to tax; government role in the management of educational institutes run by religious bodies; ban on preferential hiring within the faith, if the institute receives government funding, and so on. While some of these may make sense in principle, such as non-discriminatory hiring by institutes availing government funds, it is simply unfathomable why this ought to apply to only one religion. Further, provisions like government administrators having the final say on temple rituals of only one religion, besides indicating systemic bias, are decidedly non-secular by all standards.

This kind of State interference in religion is peculiar. There are theistic States that discriminate against religions other than the official one (think Pakistan or Saudi Arabia). There were and are theistic States that behave in a somewhat secular manner, with much greater tolerance of non-official religions (think of the late Ottoman Empire or present day Dubai). There are secular States that are perceived to exercise bias in favour of the majority religion (Turkey in recent years). But India seems to be unique—the only democratic, secular republic that meddles in the places of worship of only one religion, that of the majority population.

So, what about those other religious reforms that came about through State intervention? Surely, we must all agree that banning sati, untouchability and instant triple talaq are good things? Yes, absolutely! However, there are two distinctions between those and the restrictions at temples in Sabarimala, Puri and the like. Both are well demonstrated with examples from India as well as the US, which is the democratic republic with the oldest and deepest commitment to separation of Church and State.

First, the State has a responsibility for each citizen's individual constitutional rights that transcend the rights of the religious group to which he or she may belong. The classic example is the US SC's ruling that a child's immunization cannot be dispensed with because the adults in her religion deem it against their faith. India's prohibition on sati, caste discrimination and instant triple talaq fall in this category, making it entirely rational for the State to intervene to ensure the citizen's individual rights. These issues impact citizens in their everyday life and our Constitution mandates that the State ensure equality for all.

This idea is further embellished by a contrarian US SC ruling, entitling a baker to refuse to sell cake for same-sex weddings on the basis of his religious beliefs. While this has dismayed some, the underlying principle has a certain consistency (think of a Jewish or Muslim butcher refusing to sell pork). The disappointed couple can find an alternative baker, whereas a child whose immunization is blocked by parents on religious grounds has only the State to aid her health.

The second distinction about the State intervening in the practices at a place of worship, as opposed to citizens' daily life in the wider world, is the venue itself. While it is every citizen's prerogative to practise any religion, or none, it cannot be every individual's right to impose his version of a religion on others who profess it. Thus, while he may practise religion as he pleases in private, in a religion's place of group worship, the rituals, subject to not harming anyone, must reflect the group consensus.

Treating a place of worship like an office or a college will not work. Female college students often assert their right to wear clothing of their choice on campus, and rightly so. But no visitor to a Buddhist stupa or Sikh gurudwara—man or woman—would insist on violating their dress codes. Similarly, many mosques in the UK seat women only at the back, and while their government would not countenance such segregation in buses, it considers this the business of the congregation.

This article was first published in *The Times of India* on 24 October 2018

4

HOW TO STOP RAPES

*Death penalty is not the answer, but police and
prosecutorial reform are*

After another spate of horrific rapes of minors—some involving gruesome violence and murder—the Union government, in April 2018, finally issued an ordinance incorporating the provision of the death sentence for rapes of minor girls. This had been a long-standing demand of many agitated citizens, though there are also sceptics who doubt it will halt the epidemic.

This new ordinance is the latest example of India's penchant for compensating the lack of enforcement of various laws by introducing ever stiffer penalties in those laws, though it is oddly not gender-neutral, considering that boys also get raped. In any case, the brutality of some of the recent assaults undoubtedly qualifies as 'rarest of rare'—the SC's yardstick for awarding death sentences.

Sometimes, those additional penalties are summary—such as a mandatory arrest based on an accusation alone, even without prima facie evidence. That is the crux of an ongoing controversy, after the SC stipulated 'due process' criteria for arrests under the SC/ST PoA Act. Of course, the death penalty proviso in the new ordinance is not summary—it does require conviction by a court.

However, convictions in India—as the proverb goes—are rarer than hen's teeth. Through a triple whammy of deterioration in policing, shambolic prosecutions and abysmal backlogs in courts, the odds of justice being delivered are so low that it is a miracle that survivors and families of victims bother to report the attacks at all.

Yet, report they do, and this is happening at a rapidly rising pace. Whether you attribute the increased reporting to an actual increase in such heinous crimes (some of it surely is), or to increased societal confidence and assertiveness, the end result remains unacceptable for any civilized society, for not only are convictions far lower than in developed democracies, the reasons in India—delays, and witnesses turning hostile—are disheartening.

Ironically, the number of convictions in such cases has risen in recent years, but the far sharper increase in the number of crimes reported has meant the percentage of convictions has fallen. In 2016, convictions for crimes against women stood at 18 per cent, and those for crimes against children were only marginally better, at just under 30 per cent.

Some are sceptical of the new death penalty and believe that it can perversely lead to child rapists killing their targets more often to reduce their chances of being caught, and because the punishments are now the same anyway. However, unless most cases are speedily adjudicated, it is largely a moot point.

Reforms in Police Administration

Curbing the impunity with which assaults are happening will require delivering swift justice. The hurdles against tackling crime begin with the police having long been politicized and the reluctance of state governments to rectify that malaise. A recent Commonwealth Human Rights Initiative study concluded that not a single Indian state has fully complied with a 2006 SC judgment issuing seven directives for police reform.

Those SC directives included appointing directors-general of police in a merit-based, transparent manner; minimum tenures for senior officers; forming Police Establishment Boards for appointments, transfers and promotions; separating investigations from law and order; a board to hear public complaints against the police; and most importantly, forming State Security Commissions (SSCs) to prevent political interference.

Even states that established the all-important SSC, have done so without incorporating the stipulated checks and balances, such as having the leader of the Opposition be a member, have other independent members, and make its recommendations binding. Such truculence leads to disastrous outcomes: for instance, Odisha, which—along with Jammu & Kashmir—has not bothered to set up an SSC, saw a much higher increase of crimes against children between 2014 and 2016 (50 per cent versus 19 per cent nationally).

Contrasting this with two examples from democracies with which we have shared systemic roots, the UK and Canada, is instructive. With its 2002 Police Reform Act, the UK distributed powers between the Home Office, the local police administration, and the chief constable of the force, in order to create a buffer between the police and the State. Similarly, Canada's police system has two striking features that, if implemented here, would revolutionize India's crime-fighting. First, instead of one monolithic force, it has police forces for municipal, provincial and federal levels, with differentiated, escalating powers. Second, based on a fundamental premise that civilians must exercise oversight and control over the police, it has supervisory boards and commissions comprising civilians. These aim to shield the police from being influenced by partisan politics and to involve community members to help improve police administration.

Police reform in India needs much else besides these, but most other steps require very large allocations of funds. For example, raising India's woefully low ratio of police personnel from today's 137 per lakh of population, to the UN-recommended 222, would increase states' expenditure by tens of thousands of crores.

This is a worthwhile investment and political resolve must be garnered to commit such funds. However, meantime, the reforms in the police administration discussed here can achieve a dramatic turnaround, with little cost other than to political egos.

This article was first published in *The Times of India* on 9 May 2018

5

LET'S NOT TRIVIALIZE RAPE

The reality is that rape is a serious crime

In June 2015, the Chennai HC stunned many when it ruled that a convicted rapist of a minor be set free in order that he and the survivor—now an adult and a mother—can come to an amicable settlement. It showed that Nehru's famous observation, 'We, in India, live simultaneously in all the ages and centuries that have preceded this middle of the twentieth century,' still holds true in present-day India.

That the woman had no desire to even meet her rapist, let alone come to some arrangement with him, seemed not to have occurred to the judge, who suggested relying on arbitration under the Alternate Dispute Resolution (ADR) mechanism. That, itself, should have been worrisome since ADR, meant to bypass time-consuming and expensive litigation, is meant for civil disputes, not criminal cases.

Constitutional democracies treat crimes as not just against the individual or family or clan, but against society as a whole. In other words, unlike some traditional communities that allow 'compromises' in lieu of 'blood money' to the victim of a crime or his/her family, modern democracies are underpinned by the rule of law. Sure, some emphasize rehabilitation as much as (or more than) punishment, but, nevertheless, do not permit any kind of compromise between the perpetrator and the victim as a way out of prosecution under the law and its consequences.

What is even worse is that the judge went on to cite, as justification, the traditions of various religions in 'non-belligerent' dispute resolution. This is doubly worrisome, since HC judges are supposed to make their rulings based on the Constitution, which they have sworn to uphold, rather than on religious precedents.

Reforms Vastly Overdue

Many aspects of judicial reform are vastly overdue. These include the system for appointing judges, currently under SC review after the Parliament's passage of the NJAC. Also, large funding increases are urgently needed in order to dramatically raise the number of judges, along with the necessary infrastructure.

India has an extremely low ratio of judges to population, compared to developed countries, which is a major bottleneck in the delivery of justice. Further, there is a need for matching reforms in policing and other related areas. All of these require either time-consuming consensus building across the political spectrum, very large increases in funding, or both. However, what can happen even without such fundamental changes is the streamlining of intra-judiciary guidelines and principles based on SC precedents.

Fortunately, the SC itself, as the last recourse, keeps righting the course of justice from flagrant detours. Just a week after the Madras HC judgment, it overruled a similar Madhya Pradesh HC decision in which the judge had shown leniency to a convicted rapist, citing that he had almost finalized a compromise settlement with the parents of the victim—a seven-year-old! The SC noted, 'We would like to clearly state that in a case of rape or attempt of rape, the conception of compromise under no circumstances can really be thought of.'

It is high time that the already overburdened SC should not be additionally burdened with routinely correcting such obvious miscarriages of justice. In fact, HCs should also not intervene to reconsider convictions, unless there are specific circumstances justifying it. In other words, the leeway given to HC benches to intervene in these matters ought to be tightly circumscribed by the highest court.

However, let there not be an impression that such wastage of courts' time and resources on already settled principles of justice weighs only against one gender. Cursory googling throws up a number of false rape cases, from the malicious and completely fabricated, to the more common type where a jilted woman alleges rape only to make a recalcitrant lover honour his promise to marry her.

In fact, it is in dealing with such alleged 'rapes' resulting from broken promises of marriage that many judges have fallen prey to their kinder instincts in facilitating reconciliations. And they are not alone, since there are, at least, as many reported instances of the police acting as matchmakers and marriage counsellors.

Although some think that there is nothing wrong in such well-meaning indulgence by cops and judges, the reality is that rape is a serious crime that simply must not be trivialized. Just like there must not be any leniency for convicted rapists based on any 'compromise' with survivors, neither should there be any tolerance for fake allegations of rape, and especially not for perjury before a court.

Lately, some courts have started taking a stricter view—for instance, the additional sessions judge in Delhi in 2014, who acquitted an alleged rapist, and noted that the complainant and her husband were fit to be put on trial for perjury. Nevertheless, that is far from the norm.

The basic concepts—that it is not rape unless there has been coercion or lack of consent; that sex with mutual consent is not rape even if a promise of marriage is subsequently broken; that sex with a minor is statutory rape, irrespective of consent; and that rape is not a crime that can be settled with a compromise—are all well-established principles that should no longer require SC intervention to get lower courts to understand.

This article was first published in *The Times of India* on 8 July 2015

6

MILES TO GO

*Mass starvation has become a thing of the past in
Odisha, but other horrors remain*

Last week, two shocking videos from the interiors of Odisha
went viral, showing how far we still have to go to overcome the
depredations of poverty, and the governance challenge of treating
the poor with dignity in life and death.

In one, a man called Dana Majhi was seen, accompanied by
his young daughter, carrying his dead wife's body for the lack of
a hearse at the government medical facility where she had died
of tuberculosis. They had reportedly trudged 10 km before being
filmed by a TV reporter, who also arranged a vehicle for them.
The second was even more horrifying, showing workers at another
government hospital breaking the bones of a deceased woman called
Salamani Barik, so that her body could be more easily bundled and
carried, again for the lack of a hearse.

Ironically, the Odisha government had been working for months
on a scheme called 'Mahaprayana', to provide free hearses at district
government hospitals. It was launched as scheduled, on the day after
the first video was telecast, with the inauguration of twelve of the
planned forty new hearses.

But the issue goes far beyond infrastructural shortcomings,
though, of course, that remains a key bottleneck. The shortage of
hearses, though a matter of much frustration in rural areas, has
usually been somewhat compensated by the use of ambulances
and other government vehicles for the purpose. In fact, the '108'
nationwide ambulance service has been widely hailed as particularly
well run in the state. The issue, demonstrated by these horrific

examples, is apathy and brazen disregard for the basic human courtesies that government employees ought to extend to citizens. When asked by the media after the first incident, Odisha CM Naveen Patnaik said, 'It is very distressing; we have ordered an inquiry and stringent action will be taken against those who are responsible.' Going by his past track record of initiating action against errant officials—including not just the usual suspensions or transfers, but also sackings, confiscation of corruptly acquired property, etc.—this should be taken seriously. However, the revulsion felt by millions who saw those videos will not go away easily. Such horrifying depredations hark back to the '80s image of desperately poor Odias, especially from the Kalahandi-Bolangir-Koraput districts, selling their children for a pittance in order to make ends meet. Although Odisha still is one of the poorer states in the country, the full picture is rather more complex.

In recent years, along with Bihar, Madhya Pradesh, Rajasthan and other formerly laggard states, Odisha has finally begun to catch up to the national average on many parameters. Economically, the gross state domestic production grew at 8.4 per cent in 2006–10 and 7.2 per cent in 2011–13, both of which are near or above the national average. Further, this is projected to increase to 10.5 per cent for the period 2014–20.

Though one of the challenges of higher growth is an increased disparity between the poor and the better off, Odisha seems to have done reasonably well on this front—for instance, as per the latest available census, between 2004 and 2011, Odisha recorded the highest drop in the percentage of population below the poverty line of any Indian state—25 per cent. That took its share of BPL population to 32.6 per cent, taking it out of the group of the five worst states.

Nevertheless, this must be seen in the context of enormous historical baggage. With a third of the population still desperately poor, the state still has staggering challenges to overcome. Though several socio-economic indices, such as malnutrition, gender ratio, literacy and access to drinking water, are now at, or better than, the national average, that average itself is well short of global standards. And many are below it, including infant and maternal mortality, open defecation and per capita income. Finally, poverty among the nearly 1 crore adivasi citizenry is still sharply higher than the national average.

The governance challenge is intricately linked to this ongoing transition. It is irrefutable that better governance standards are correlated to economic development and improving income patterns. In fact, they bolster each other, being cause and effect by turns.

This is where political will and stability can be a crucial catalyst. Surely, the improvements that have happened so far couldn't have happened in the absence of will. And Odisha certainly has seen stability, with the present CM now in his fourth consecutive term. Yet, this time frame itself must be seen as something akin to the midpoint of a transition, with miles to go before certain minimum standards are achieved across the board.

While some aspects of Odisha's image have changed—for instance, starvation-related deaths are now horrifying exceptions, unlike the hundreds of cases that used to take place routinely, every year—there still remain other aspects that remind us of the long road ahead. And in present-day India, with a ubiquitous media, a much larger middle class and global aspirations, every such individual atrocity will matter—as it should.

The rest of this transition will not get any easier, requiring even more political will. Administrative reform to emphasize outcomes, accountability in place of hierarchy and red tape, a dramatic boosting of investment and skilling, and the use of Aadhaar and similar initiatives to alleviate dire poverty—these solutions are much easier said than done, but are not rocket science.

This article was first published in *The Times of India* on 31 August 2016

7

FIFTY SHADES OF GREY

*We sometimes condone vigilantism due to system
breakdown, but that's a slippery slope*

The 2016 incident where four men from the SCs' community
were stripped, tied and beaten for skinning a dead cow was
condemnable. It was criticized all round—in the media, in drawing
rooms, during tea stall conversations, and in the Parliament.
Thankfully, with one sorry exception, not even habitual 'foot in
mouth' experts tried to defend the indefensible.

Yet, the discourse was partisan, as is now the norm for almost
every issue in these contentious times. Allegations flew back and
forth about whether what is being called 'cow vigilantism' was
happening more in certain states, or across the country, irrespective
of the party in government; and so did the statistics, on the string
of such incidents in recent months versus the voluminous data of
unrelenting atrocities upon SCs for decades.

Heinous and commonplace as such atrocities continue to be,
vigilantism is a wider phenomenon, for it is not just limited to
attacks on people of any one caste or religion, and its underlying
causes bring into question the belief in our system of governance,
which is the glue binding us together as a nation.

The unceasing vigilante incidents routinely reported in the
media are a varied lot. Most often, they involve people taking the
law into their own hands to deliver instant justice to alleged robbers
and rapists. However, there is also vigilantism to enforce cultural
mores that are not enshrined in the law, such as rulings by Khap
panchayats, fatwas by clerics, and atavistic ideas of family honour.

Both kinds of vigilantism—'speeding up' the consequences of

breaking the law, and enforcing ideas not supported by the law—are illegal and unacceptable. This is because of the principle of due process, hard-earned over centuries of evolving civilizations.

All democracies guarantee some form of due process, which assures that no matter how terrible a crime that someone is accused of, he/she cannot be punished arbitrarily or summarily. Instead, the accused is presumed innocent until proven guilty in court. India's Constitution, too, guarantees that 'No person shall be deprived of his life or personal liberty except according to a procedure established by law.'

Of course, even now, there are autocracies where due process is either non-existent or a mere formality. Who hasn't heard of swift and brutal punishments delivered in non-democratic countries around the world, like Saudi Arabia and China? They do have some advantages, though, such as far lower crime rates. Some Indians yearn for that safety, and even say they would not mind giving up some of the freedoms that are taken for granted. However, that kind of blithe wish for a 'benevolent dictatorship' does not recognize that such dispensations often turn out to be far from benevolent. Moreover, we Indians are much too individualistic to give up many freedoms for long. Most importantly, it is actually many democracies—like Japan, Norway and South Korea—which dominate the ranks of low-crime nations.

What Motivates Vigilantism

To overcome vigilantism, it is worth trying to understand what motivates it. Listen to Sampat Pal Devi, former leader of the Uttar Pradesh-based Gulabi Gang, a pink sari-wearing, lathi-wielding group of women fighting against gender violence, sometimes described as the largest female vigilante group in the world: 'This country is ruled by men... It's no use asking them for help. We women must fight our own battles ourselves.'

So, is vigilante justice ever legally or morally justified? According to American academic Hillel Gray, 'Certainly, yes. In the absence of a legal order, or when legal authorities are blatantly unjust, it can be ethically appropriate to act without authorization of the law.'

In a week that has seen another horrific gang rape—of a mother and her minor daughter, whose family was waylaid on a highway—who among us can ignore the plight of victims and their families? The apathy, cruelty and enormous delays of our criminal justice system are simply unconscionable. When justice is frustrated more often than it is delivered, it is natural for faith in the rule of law to erode.

No wonder, then, that there is so much impunity among criminals. Equally, we should not be surprised by incidents like that in March 2015, when a mob of thousands broke into Dimapur's central jail, dragged out an alleged rapist who had been arrested, and beat him to death.

Our collective outrage at the state of affairs has, by now, reached a crucial fork in the road. One turn, where we begin to tolerate vigilantism because of the visible breakdown of the system, can yield a temporary sense of, somehow, 'justice' having been done; but this is a slippery slope, with ever-diminishing returns, towards total anarchy.

The other choice is the far more difficult one, of facing up to the enormous challenges of setting right what is still, of course, salvageable. However, there are no glib answers or quick solutions. It will take lakhs of crores of rupees to bring about the necessary judicial, police and prosecution reforms, and even that, though desperately needed, will take years to yield results.

Meanwhile, the appeal of vigilantism must be countered by the very real risk that, without the checks and balances of due process, it will inevitably be misused. Even Gulabi Gang has reportedly removed Sampat Devi, allegedly for offering the group's services on hire as mercenaries.

This article was first published in *The Times of India* on 4 August 2016

8

NAME THE PROBLEM

The world must support those within Islam,
who are speaking up for reform

To keep insisting that terrorism has nothing to do with religion after every new jihadi atrocity is no longer tenable. It is galling for millions of people—not just Indians but around the world—when this clichéd phrase is parroted even as reports go viral of the attackers' in-your-face assertion of religion.

Followers of most major religions have killed in the name of their faith, but as author and TV host Fareed Zakaria has said, 'The next time you hear of a terror attack—no matter where, no matter what the circumstances—you will likely think to yourself, "It's Muslims again". And you will probably be right.'

However, the vast majority of the world's 1.6 billion Muslims do not consider jihadi killers as representative of their religion. They stress that such killers are violating some of Islam's basic tenets of compassion, and that most victims of such terrorism are Muslims. The spate of murderous jihadi attacks during the Islamic holy month of Ramadan (or Ramzan in South Asia), has been denounced by many Muslims as desecrating their faith.

Most world leaders echo these sentiments. With few exceptions, it is standard for politicians everywhere to publicly say that jihadis do not represent the religion they claim to. Yet, that extreme political correctness of denying any connection with religion, even as terrorists shout religious slogans and test Quranic knowledge while slaughtering victims, has led to growing public anger.

Another common refrain is that only moderate Muslims can respond to this 'internal' challenge in Islam. However, when they do respond, they often face extreme hostility, not only from other Muslims, but also, shockingly, even from secular institutions of the media as well as universities. There are many documented instances of these, even in that Mecca of free speech, the US.

Many disillusioned moderate Muslims have either stopped believing (at great risk, since jihadis violently enforce Islam's intolerance of apostasy), or have resigned themselves into quiescence. It is these voices—and not just the good Samaritans who empathize with victims, but dare not push for religious reforms—that deserve the support of those who are truly secular.

After the Boston Marathon bombings, Pakistani-Canadian writer Ali A. Rizvi wrote,

> The 'anything but jihad' brigade is out in full force again. If the perpetrators of such attacks say they were influenced by politics (or) nationalism…we take them at face value. But when they consistently cite their religious beliefs as their central motivation, we back off, stroke our chins and suspect there *has* to be something deeper at play, a 'root cause'. It is often religion itself…that is the root cause.

Speaking Up for Reform

The sort of aforementioned candour is lacking among most mainstream commentators in modern, liberal democracies today. Calling out jihadi terrorism is inhibited for fear of being labelled 'prejudiced', 'Islamophobic' or, oddly, even 'racist'.

The holy texts of most ancient religions—Judaism, Christianity, Islam and Hinduism—contain exhortations to love, tolerance and kindliness on the one hand, and revenge, misogyny and violence, on the other. Barack Obama has reminded the world 'that during the Crusades and the Inquisition, people committed terrible deeds in the name of Christ'.

Virtually, all major religions have had fanatical, murderous adherents. Even in modern times, there are several examples of religious killings besides those by Islamists—for instance, by Buddhists in Sri Lanka and Myanmar, and Christian abortion-clinic bombers in the US. India has seen terrorism by Sikh extremists, and among Hindus, there is Dara Singh, convicted for life for killing an Australian missionary and his children. Other instances of alleged Hindu terrorism from 2007 to 2010 (Samjhauta, Malegaon, Ajmer) are being adjudicated in courts.

However, on the basis of sheer scale of the number of attacks and fatalities, nothing comes close to jihadi terrorism. Even 'traditional', non-religious, left-wing extremists like Germany's Baader-Meinhof Group, Italy's Red Brigades, the Revolutionary Armed Forces of Colombia–People's Army, Peru's Shining Path and our very own Naxalites are now either defunct or well past their peak.

The numbers speak for themselves: the 2015 statistics cited by political scientist Ian Bremmer show that the world's top terrorist organizations are the Islamic State (8,420 fatalities), Boko Haram (6,299), Taliban (5,215) and al-Shabaab (1,586). That al-Qaeda doesn't even rank any more shows how exponential the growth of Islamist radicalization has been.

Ayaan Hirsi Ali, a bestselling author and Somali refugee has said,

> It simply will not do for Muslims to claim that their religion has been 'hijacked' by extremists. The killers of Islamic State and Boko Haram cite the same religious texts that every other Muslim in the world considers sacrosanct... The biggest obstacle to change within the Muslim world is suppression of critical thinking.

It is not that other religions have sanitized their religious texts, but they have coped with modernity better. As Zakaria puts it, 'Islamic terrorists don't just hate America or the West. They hate the modern world.' For jihadi terrorism to subside, this must change.

What the world needs now is not more platitudes and political correctness. It needs support for those within Islam, who are speaking up for reform and adaption to modernity. Otherwise, the sacrifice of many brave Muslims who stand up to terrorists—like Faraaz Hossain, who died in the Dhaka attack because he refused to abandon his friends—will go in vain.

This article was first published in *The Times of India* on 6 July 2016

9

HYPOCRISY ON FREE SPEECH

The free speech debate is complicated by the broad range of taboos, as also the hypocrisy in supporting free speech on others' taboos, but not one's own

A valid argument can be made about the Indian establishment's instinctive use and misuse of colonial-era laws like sedition, but not if it is partisan; for, it is disingenuous to claim, as some have, that somehow it is only now that the government is clamping down on free speech. Have we so quickly forgotten the 2012 arrests of a cartoonist for sedition, and that of college students for 'offensive' SM posts?

Since the protest rallies at Jawaharlal Nehru University (JNU) in 2016, the nation has been embroiled in an angry debate about freedom of expression. This is a debate worth having—indeed, it is necessary—but it needs rescuing from the political agendas of both extremes of the right and the left.

First, however, it is important to understand the historical context of this debate, and that free speech and sedition need to be considered in conjunction with blasphemy.

The modern concept of free speech evolved over several centuries in Europe, when scientists and philosophers, with their stunning discoveries and compelling arguments for reason and rationality, loosened the grip of the Church on everyday life. In the process, blasphemy—earlier, the most heinous of crimes—came to be considered as merely distasteful, rather than criminal.

Of course, even today, theocratic States like Saudi Arabia and Pakistan treat blasphemy as a crime punishable by death, but most democracies do not, and have either repealed blasphemy laws or no longer implement them, with varying degrees of freedom. For over two centuries, it is the US that has gradually developed the gold standard of these freedoms.

The US constitutional guarantee of free speech, backed by many court rulings, is near absolute, with two narrowly defined exceptions. Those exceptions impose restrictions on child pornography and the leaking of classified information compromising national security. Even burning the national flag has been held by the US SC to be permissible as an aspect of freedom of expression, and even when such inflammatory acts as burning holy books are threatened, the government can do little. Though there are laws against inciting violence, courts have ruled that there must be imminent, 'clear and present' danger for the authorities to intervene.

The US has also had several sedition laws since its inception, but many have been repealed over the centuries or overruled by courts. Those that remain, are tightly defined, differentiating 'opinion' and 'speech' from 'action'. A typical example is a 1957 US judgment 'that teaching an ideal, no matter how harmful it may seem, does not equal advocating or planning its implementation'.

These distinctions between speech and action are crucial to our debate in India. India's SC, too, has ruled in a similar vein, holding that sedition was only applicable if there was 'an incitement to violence' or 'public disorder', and that even pro-separatist slogans for Khalistan did not qualify.

A Complicated Debate

The consensus among free nations today is increasingly in favour of either repealing sedition laws or, at least, tightly limiting them to 'actions'—not 'speech'—aimed at overthrowing the State or physically facilitating rebellion or secession. India has faced such challenges within living memory, which is why it is understandable that the topic triggers raw emotions. Nevertheless, it is perfectly possible to be both revolted by some of the slogans at JNU, but still support free speech. That was Voltaire's principle, exemplified in a

1770 letter: 'I detest what you write, but I would give my life to make it possible for you to continue to write.'

The catch lies elsewhere, in that India's free speech rights are nowhere near absolute. The Constitution itself mentions a broad array of restrictions, including security, foreign relations, public order and morality. Further, though courts have repeatedly supported free speech and stretched its limits, they have also reinforced boundaries.

Groups from both the left and the right have cited free speech to advance their agenda, while also clamouring for restrictions when it doesn't suit them. On the left, for instance, some of the very people who castigated me for simply proposing a debate on Rajya Sabha's powers, and even moved a privilege motion against me, are now championing free speech at JNU, apparently without irony.

Similarly, there are reports of both left- and right-wing student groups blocking guest speakers and film screenings at JNU, the University Of Allahabad and elsewhere. Both sides accuse sections of the mainstream media of bias and being 'embedded' in the other side's ecosystem. Both sides also seem to have a love-hate relationship with SM, seeing it as a leveller that enables their stories to be told, but also of it being misused by the other side's supporters.

Across the spectrum, many believe that some subjects are taboo, especially regarding religious sentiments. The free speech debate is complicated by the broad range of taboos, as also the hypocrisy in supporting free speech on others' taboos, but not one's own.

However, free speech is not really free if it is sanitized. A crucial difference is the distinction between speech and action. The support for it should be on principle, with narrowly defined exceptions, instead of tribalism. India needs a larger group in the middle to stand up for this.

This article was first published in *The Times of India* on 16 March 2016

10

A NATIONAL PRIORITY

It's time for the government to get serious about tackling the exploitation of labourers

Harvard scholar Siddharth Kara estimates that there are between 1.8 crore to 2.25 crore bonded labourers in the world, with 85 per cent of them in South Asia alone. He estimates that India itself has upwards of 60 per cent of the world's bonded labour, a statistic amounting to 1.07 crore people.

As we grapple with the enormity of this challenge, the annual World Day against Trafficking in Persons was marked on 30 July. Every year, millions of children, men and women are trafficked and exploited for profit. Unwitting victims are pushed into hazardous occupations that leave them with little avenues for exit, apart from consequences for their health and well-being. Yet, despite widespread recognition of the crimes committed by unscrupulous actors in our own society, concrete action has lacked considerably.

As a public representative from the state of Odisha, I have personally interacted with many who have been pushed into bonded labour, lured by agents and middlemen, with the promise of jobs and a steady stream of income to send home. In a welcome development in 2015, around 748 victims of labour trafficking from my home state of Odisha, working in brick kilns across Tamil Nadu, Andhra Pradesh and Karnataka, were rescued by the International Justice Mission, a global organization that protects the poor from violence throughout the developing world.

Odisha is one of the major source-states for this form of exploitation and the 748 rescued labourers made for only 0.0044 per cent of this serious problem. In recent years, I have visited brick kilns in Telangana's Ranga Reddy district and talked to the various stakeholders, including migrant workers, state government officials, brick kiln owners and their agents, as well as activists and NGOs. Nevertheless, such visits only prove to highlight an already recognized issue and any positive outcomes have, so far, only scratched the surface of the problem. We need to accept this reality of debt bondage faced by millions in our country and rather than brushing it under the carpet, serious questions need to be asked with regard to the enforcement mechanism of already existing protective laws.

It is important to note that even labour trafficking and bonded labour, though a pervasive and long-functioning concept in our country, experience changes in pattern. The traffickers have been quick to adapt and continue with their operations. It is my experience that, from Odisha, migration caused by everyday desperation has been on the decline—for example, starvation is no longer a pressing issue in Odisha as opposed to a decade or so ago, and is contributing less to labour trafficking on account of strong economic growth and robust social safety net programmes for the poor. However, there is still a paucity of higher-paying livelihoods, providing leverage for traffickers to nudge people to explore opportunities in nearby states. In light of this change, traffickers now extend a lump sum payment of around ₹13,000 per family member.

The labourers are charged interest for the upfront lump sum payment and the weekly allowance, which is then deducted from their wage earnings. In sum, the net payment received by the labourer is lower than what was promised/expected. Moreover, this net value is below the minimum wage set by the state. Labourers do not have any recourse besides fearing for their and their families' lives if they choose to speak up.

I do not need to elaborate on the injustices committed, as there is sufficient evidence to demonstrate how labourers are exploited, forced to live in hovels, and denied minimum wages and their basic human rights. Indeed, I have heard of such injustices first-hand. I hope our enforcement mechanism would be strengthened in consideration of the adversarial consequences that are imposed on those forced in to bonded labour.

The Barriers

It is important to note that it is not just adults (men or women) who are affected adversely, but children as well.

Labourers and their families are trapped in unliveable conditions—sometimes with even children being forced to do back-breaking work for long hours; physically and sexually abused; and prevented from returning home. Moreover, brick kilns see seasonal employment and the children of labourers are forced out of school. Language can be a barrier to schooling, as such migration occurs between states. Though some state laws require employers of migrant labour to arrange for teaching the children in their mother tongue, enforcement is inconsistent.

Thus, our efforts require greater cooperation between state governments to combat this menace, especially with regard to inter-state labour movements, registering and monitoring agents and middlemen, and rescues. Labour trafficking engages more than a single state's jurisdiction and it is imperative that cooperation is strengthened by way of the regular interaction of officials, defining definitive roles for all state governments involved and ensuring speedy rehabilitation.

The Centre can ensure that the release of funds to the state for rehabilitation efforts are done without delay so that those affected do not return to bonded labour. Most importantly, let this issue not be reduced to being the burden of a particular state. It must be understood as a national priority to help those already facing enormous challenges in their everyday life.

This article was first published in *Daily Mail Online* on 31 July 2015

11

SOME ARE MORE EQUAL THAN OTHERS

Kalam stood in line; when will our netas follow?

My respect for former President Dr A.P.J. Adbul Kalam has gone up after he refused to object on being frisked by an airline security. However, the furore it created was inevitable. The outrage over his frisking has a deep-rooted connection with a still-fragile, post-colonial mindset: the fact that the airline was an American one—cue sharp intake of breath—made it that much worse. Nevertheless, despite many Indians' gossamer-thin skin at any real or perceived slight by foreigners, this is a good opportunity to re-examine our own assumptions about special privileges.

After initially holding firm that it was only abiding by the US Transport Security Administration rules, which do not recognize an Indian ex-president as exempt from frisking, the airline is subsequently reported to have apologized. This was entirely predictable, not just because there is an Indian law exempting ex-presidents from security checks, but also because the civil aviation minister personally assured the Parliament that the recalcitrant airline would be brought to book.

That is as it should be—Indian laws and rules should be taken seriously by any entity operating in India. However, my cavil is with the law itself. Why should an ever expanding list of VIPs be exempt from security checks at the airport? Why should we still have a feudal mindset that our ruling elite be treated differently from the average citizen?

It has sometimes been argued that this mindset, more than just being a feudal relic, also specifically reflects a Third World mindset. The logic goes that Third World countries are only tolerable (to the elite) when there are special privileges to shield them from the rigours of everyday life in such countries. It is a vestige of twentieth-century India, which still lingers on even as the country itself is trying to come to grips with the kind of mindset that is more suited for an emerging twenty-first-century power.

When India became independent after years of foreign domination, it was but natural that the nation was insecure about itself, and not confident of competing with the world. This bruised self-esteem, combined with the power of democracy, unleashed forces hitherto unknown. Populism, which was fairly useless until independence, became a potent force for acquiring and retaining power. Policies to facilitate real development were subjugated to those that played to the gallery.

India settled into a cycle of low growth, low investment and a slow reduction of poverty, which was far from ideal for the aam aadmi, but had little downside for the elite. Particularly during the '60s through the early '90s, the Indian ruling cabal of netas, babus and well-connected businessmen developed a comfortable, if incestuous, formula for mutual gratification, and special privileges were a fundamental part of that formula. These ranged from the substantive to the frivolous and included special access to otherwise restricted goodies—think imported luxury cars for businessmen. Netas and babus got to live in heritage buildings in areas that were exempt from power cuts, and would drive in ubiquitous Ambassador cars with beacon lights. Further, they never had to stand in line for anything.

This clubby existence reinforced a feudal, Third World mindset. Worries about '*bijli, sadak, pani*' (electricity, road, water) were not top-of-the-mind, since those were indeed not the hardships to which netas and babus could relate. The hardships with which they could relate all had to do with the pecking order: the correct colour of beacon light for their car, the higher level of security detail, and arrangements to bypass queues of all kinds.

Things have been changing; just not fast enough. Democracy has flourished to an extent that voters who were earlier content with identity politics and willing to buy into populist slogans are increasingly rewarding development. Liberalization and economic growth have made available to the hoi polloi what earlier only the exalted could have—for instance, when was the last time you needed a neta or a babu's clout to get a phone connection on the same day? These things have started impacting cultural mores as well: an entire generation of Indians has now grown up without the core belief that a bribe is necessary to get that phone connection.

This kind of basic belief system that bribes or special privileges are unnecessary to get access to a wide array of daily needs and wants is essential for us to transition to a First World mindset. For that to happen, there are still large swathes of our economy that need to be unshackled from the '60s and '70s-style governance that fosters shortages and a patronage system. An India where the average citizen can get access to education, health, jobs and quick legal redress without patronage or bribes—all possible in our lifetimes with sensible policymaking—will be a country that will have no room left for a feudal or Third World mindset.

In the meantime, it is only when most of the ruling elite are not exempt from airport security checks that there will be greater urgency to reform and streamline it. Our long list of those exempted should be trimmed down, like most First World countries, to a very, very short list. The ideal list would exempt only the serving president and heads of each pillar of the Constitution: the executive (PM), the judicial (chief justice), and the legislative (vice president and speaker). Until that happens, we must applaud the likes of Dr Kalam who don't bother about such petty privileges.

This article was first published in *The Indian Express* on 25 July 2009

EPILOGUE

As I come to the end of this book, India is less than six months away from the 2019 general elections. Like each of its predecessors, this too will set a new record for the largest number of citizens ever to exercise their franchise in a democracy.

Much in this book both celebrates this largest democracy that the world has ever seen and points out its systemic shortcomings and calls for reforms. In doing so, I tried to let candour be the leitmotif, and use benchmarking (a skill honed from my management days) against other democracies as a key method of looking for solutions.

I am a firm believer of not only cherishing our glorious heritage of many millennia, but also not being sucked into a feeling of hubris, thinking that the rest of the world has nothing to teach us. In fact, while all humans are unique, human societies often have recurrent themes—experiences that transcend geography, history, culture and time. In other words, India can teach the world a lot, but also learn much from others' experiences, especially those democracies that may have experienced similar challenges.

My chosen path in politics has also been to avoid knee-jerk responses in favour of more considered ones. My fraternity often sees, or at least espouses, black-and-white alternatives. I tend to think that there are shades of grey that are interesting, worth exploring and, ultimately, more likely to yield practical solutions.

This is sometimes considered a weakness—as losing an opportunity to amplify differences in order to leverage one's own position. But that too, is a matter of perspective. Amplifying differences can be an easy shortcut to getting attention—and it is a tactic used by all sides, not just any particular political grouping, as some might have you believe. But in democracies, lasting solutions only emerge from bridging differences, even if that has to wait until power is gained through less temperate means.

To maintain a moderate approach in both the quest for power and its later exercise in government, is, of course, the ultimate political tightrope walk. Though not commonplace, it is not unheard of either. Every now and then, political figures appear, who have managed to pull off this combination.

Finally, in *Lutyens' Maverick*, I have been both candid and forthright, yet also attempted to bridge uneasy differences with empathy and flexibility. To what extent I have succeeded in this is, of course, for you to judge. For my part, it will be reward enough if any of these arguments validated or provided support for views that had been developed on instinct alone. And indeed, it would be even more gratifying if, at least on occasion, I have provoked you to either reconsider earlier positions or think them through again.

Apart from the names I have acknowledged in the introduction, Rupa Publications's Senior Commissioning Editor assigned to handle this book, Yamini Chowdhury, was outstanding. She was focused, persuasive and assertive, but also flexible and reasonable. In addition, one of my best sources of feedback during writing was my wife Jagi Mangat Panda, with her combination of encouragement and brutally frank critiques.

There have been many others who inspired, encouraged, supported and even cajoled me into writing—they are too numerous to list, and include family members, friends, colleagues and also people I met at conferences, weddings and while travelling. I thank them all.

As mentioned in the introduction, there have also been numerous young men and women who have worked with me, and their spirited participation in brainstorming and argumentative sessions have helped me to pick topics on which to write, hone my thoughts and express myself with greater accuracy. Despite that, if any errors have crept in, they are mine alone.

Of the many names in this category, I must mention, in particular, Shruti Jagirdar, Rohit Kumar, Iravati Damle, Yashita

Jhurani, Jasmine Luthra, Anil Sebastian Pulickel and Nayantara Narayan. In addition, my team members, Suvendu Pani, Vaneeta Naik, Jyoti Ghose and Deepak Panda, from time to time, succeeded in staving off the unending diversions an active politician faces, block time on my schedule and nudge me to write. Thank you, all.

GLOSSARY

A.P.J. Adbul Kalam
Aadhaar
Aam Aadmi Party (AAP)
Adi Shankaracharya
Afzal Guru
Air India
Ajit Doval
al-Shabaab
al-Qaeda
Alternate Dispute Resolution (ADR)
Amazon
Ambassador
America Online
American Enterprise Institute
Annual Status of Education Report
artificial intelligence (AI)
Arun Jaitley
Arvind Kejriwal
Arya Samaj Shuddhi movement
Apple
Aseem Trivedi
Asian Infrastructure Investment Bank
Association of Southeast Asian Nations
Atal Bihari Vajpayee

Baader-Meinhof Group
Bahujan Samaj Party
Barack Obama

Below Poverty Line (BPL)
Belt and Road Initiative
Beti Bachao Beti Padhao
Bharatiya Janata Party (BJP)
Bhimrao Ramji Ambedkar
big data
Bill Clinton
Biju Janata Dal (BJD)
black money
blasphemy
Brandenburg test
BRICS
British Broadcasting Corporation (BBC)
Boko Haram
Bruno Le Maire

C. Rajagopalachari
Cato the Younger
child pornography
crony capitalism
Code of Criminal Procedure (CCP)
Commonwealth Human Rights Initiative
Communist Party of India
CompuServe
Conduct of Election Rules, 1961
Congress
Council of States
cow vigilantism

Daily News and Analysis
Dainik Jagran
Dawood Ibrahim
demonetization
Deng Xiaoping
Development Partnership Administration (DPA)

Digital India
Direct Benefits Transfer for LPG (DBTL)
Donald Trump

Ease of Doing Business (EoDB) index
East India Company
Economic Survey-II
Education for All Development Index
Election Commission (EC)
electronic voting machines (EVMs)
Export Oriented Units

Facebook
Fitch
Free Basics
Foreign direct investment (FDI)

General Headquarters (GHQ)
Give It Up
Google
Goods and Services Tax (GST)
Government of India Act
Gross Domestic Product (GDP)
Gulabi Gang

H.D. Deve Gowda
Hardik Patel
Haqqani network
Heritage Foundation
Hillary Clinton
Hindu Marriage Act
Hindustan Times
HMT watches
House of Lords

IBM
Imran Khan
Income Tax (IT) Act
Inder Kumar Gujral
India Today
Indian Administrative Service (IAS)
Indian Telegraph Act
Indira Gandhi
Indo-Pak Track II dialogue
Indrajit Gupta Committee
Information Technology Act
International Justice Mission
International Monetary Fund (IMF)
Internet Corporation for Assigned Names and Numbers
Interstate Commerce Act
Islamic State
IT Appellate Tribunals

Jaish-e-Mohammed
Jan Dhan
Janata Dal
Jawaharlal Nehru
Jehangir Tata
Judicial Appointments Commission (JAC)
Julius Caesar

Kautilya
King Canute

Lashkar-e-Taiba
Lakshmi Mittal
Land Acquisition, Rehabilitation and Resettlement (LARR) Act
Law Commission
Lehman Brothers
lever voting machine

Li Keqiang
liberalization
Line of Control (LoC)
liquid petroleum gas (LPG)
Lok Sabha

Mahabharata
Mahaprayana
Mahatma Gandhi National Rural Employment Guarantee Act
(MGNREGA)
Mahindra
Make in India
Manmohan Singh
Margaret Thatcher
Matteo Renzi
Microsoft
Moody's
Motilal
mutually assured destruction (MAD)

N.T. Rama Rao
Nandan Nilekani
Nara Chandrababu Naidu
Narendra Modi
National Association of Software and Services Companies
National Crime Records Bureau
National Democratic Alliance
National Judicial Appointments Commission (NJAC)
National Institute of Public Finance and Policy (NIPFP)
National Institution for Transforming India (NITI Aayog)
National Manufacturing Policy
National Optical Fibre Network
NATO (North Atlantic Treaty Organization)
Naxalites
Naveen Patnaik

Nawaz Sharif
Nirbhaya
Nitish Kumar

OBC (other backward class)
Ola
Organisation of Economic Co-operation and Development (OECD)
Outlook

P.V. Narasimha Rao
Panchayati Raj
Palaniappan Chidambaram
paper ballots
Parliamentary Standing Committee on Personnel, Public Grievances,
    Law and Justice
Patidar movement
Permanent Account Number (PAN)
Planning Commission
Pranab Mukherjee
Program for International Student Assessment (PISA)
Progressive Era
Prohibition of Child Marriage Act (PCMA)
Protection of Children from Sexual Offences Act
proto-parliament
public distribution system (PDS)
Public-Private Partnerships (PPPs)
public sector undertaking (PSU)
Punch-card voting machines

Rahul Gandhi
Rajiv Aarogya Raksha plan
Rajiv Gandhi
Rajya Sabha
Ramayana
Red Brigades

Regional Comprehensive Economic Partnership
remonetization
Representation of the People Act (RoPA), 1951
reservations
Reserve Bank of India (RBI)
Revolutionary Armed Forces of Colombia–People's Army
Right to Education Act (RTE)
Right to Information Act (RTI)
Ronald Reagan
'root cause' theory

Samajwadi Party (SP)
Sampat Pal Devi
Sarojini Naidu
Sarva Shiksha Abhiyan
Scheduled Castes (SCs)
Scheduled Caste and Scheduled Tribe (Prevention of Atrocities)
    [SC/ST PoA]
Scheduled Tribes (STs)
sedition
Shah Bano
Shanghai Cooperation Organisation
Shashi Tharoor
Shining Path
Shivraj Singh Chouhan
Silicon Valley
Sivan Pillai
social media (SM)
Sonia Gandhi
South Asian Association for Regional Cooperation
Special Economic Zones
Special Marriage Act
Standard & Poor's (S&P)
Standard Oil Company
State Security Commissions (SSCs)

Subhas Chandra Bose
Supreme Court
Swachh Bharat
Swami Lakshmanananda Saraswati
Swami Shraddhanand

T.N. Iyer Seshan
Taliban
Talwars
Taslima Nasreen
Tata
Telecom Regulatory Authority of India
Telugu Desam Party
The Asian Age
The Economist
The Indian Express
The Times of India
The Wall Street Journal
The Wizard of Oz
Theodore Roosevelt
Trinamool Congress
triple talaq

Uber
uniform civil code (UCC)
Unique Identification programme
UN Convention on Elimination of All Forms of Discrimination
    against Women
UN Educational, Scientific and Cultural Organization
UN International Children's Emergency Fund (UNICEF)
UN Security Council (UNSC)
United Nations (UN)
United Progressive Alliance (UPA)
Universal Basic Income (UBI)
Universal Service Obligation Fund (USOF)

US Dodd-Frank Wall Street Reform and Consumer Protection Act
US Transport Security Administration

Vasundhara Raje
Vatican Radio
Voter Verifiable Paper Audit Trail

Wall Street
Watson AI system
Westminster model
World Bank
World Day against Trafficking in Persons
World War II

Y Combinator
Yakub Memon